THE VIKING

saga one

Viking Pride

Christopher Tebbetts

PUFFIN BOOKS

For Jonathan

PUFFIN BOOKS
Published by Penguin Group
Penguin Young Readers Group,
345 Hudson Street, New York, New York 10014, U.S.A.
Penguin Books Ltd, 80 Strand, London WC2R ORL, England
Penguin Books Australia Ltd, 250 Camberwell Road, Camberwell, Victoria 3124, Australia
Penguin Books Canada Ltd, 10 Alcorn Avenue, Toronto, Ontario, Canada M4V 3B2
Penguin Books (N.Z.) Ltd, 182-190 Wairau Road, Auckland 10, New Zealand

Published by Puffin Books, a division of Penguin Young Readers Group, 2003

1 3 5 7 9 10 8 6 4 2

 Text copyright © 17th Street Productions,
an Alloy Inc. company, 2003
All rights reserved
Book design by Jim Hoover
The text of this book is set in Arrus BT

LIBRARY OF CONGRESS CATALOGING-IN-PUBLICATION DATA
Tebbetts, Christopher.
The Viking saga one: Viking pride / by Christopher Tebbetts.
p. cm.—(The Viking)
Sequel: The Viking saga two: the quest for faith.
Summary: While reluctantly attending a Vikings football game with his father,
fourteen-year-old Zack Gilman finds himself transported to ninth-century Scandinavia
amongst Vikings that look like people he knows and who see him as the fulfillment
of a prophecy that will help them solve the riddle of Yggdrasil's chest.
[1. Time travel—Fiction. 2. Vikings—Fiction. 3. Mythology, Norse—Fiction. 4. Fathers and
sons—Fiction.] I. Title. II. Series.
PZ7.T2235Vi 2003 [Fic]—dc21 2002036875
ISBN 0-14-250029-1

Printed in the United States of America

PROLOGUE

Graaaarggghhhh!

The mob roared as it closed in on Zack. He didn't see faces or arms or legs. He just saw one giant, swarming mass, with swords, barbed spears, and axes swinging in all directions.

GRAAAARGGHHH!

He dove out of the way just in time. The mob flew past, punishing the ground where Zack had been standing two seconds before. It was as if they had come out of nowhere, several dozen of them, shields waving and blades slicing the air. They rumbled over the crest of a hill and disappeared.

Zack sat up and spit out a mouthful of snow. He shook his head, figuring his brain was starting to freeze along with the rest of him.

Did I just imagine that?

An even louder roar than before sounded from some-where out of sight.

I guess not.

Keeping low to the ground, Zack stole to the crest of the hill and looked down at the field below.

The mob that had just passed him was joining up with

another insane-looking group of oddly dressed men. Above the rattle of chain mail and the rhythmic pounding of swords against round wooden shields, their yells and growls filled the air. There were maybe a hundred of them in all. They lined up to face a strange-looking group on the far end of the field.

The other side wore even weirder clothes: some sort of fur cloaks, with hoods. Their faces were mostly in shadow. They pawed at the ground and looked ready to charge.

Both sides were clearly gearing up for a fight. A big one.

Zack looked from one side of the field to the other, weighing his options. He couldn't turn around. There was nowhere to go. And heading down the hill would be like walking into a meat grinder. They had enough hardware down there to kill him in fifteen different ways, a hundred times over, without breaking a sweat. Besides spears, hammers, swords, axes, bows and arrows, Zack could see several nasty-looking weapons he didn't even recognize.

And then it broke. One soldier in particular, a big man with a red beard, his eyes and nose hidden behind the mask of his helmet, let out a bloodcurdling bellow. It smashed whatever dam had been holding them back. All at once, both sides rushed onto the field like two awesome waves crashing toward each other. Zack pressed down even closer to the ground as if to keep from flying off into space. He held his breath.

In a moment, the two masses became one and the battle began. There was an immediate metallic clashing as swords met swords across the field. Everywhere, soldiers were fighting hand-to-hand and in small groups. Zack's eyes darted from skirmish to skirmish. It was more than he could take in all at once.

His gaze fell again on the tall red-bearded fighter. He and another man were directly below Zack at the bottom of the hill. The two were outnumbered but held their own, swinging in every direction. They stood back to back, fending off half a dozen enemy fighters at once. The red-bearded man swung his shield in a roundhouse move that took out two opponents with one blow. His partner crossed swords with another warrior, in a rapid-fire *ting-ting-ting* of metal.

An enemy soldier stepped into the fighting circle and swung something that looked like a large hammer on a chain, sort of like a combination of a mace and a sledgehammer. Redbeard took a blow to the chest and staggered to the side, falling onto one knee. His helmet slipped off, revealing a bloodied scowling face. The enemy soldier raised his sword high over the man's head.

No way. Not possible. Error.

Before Zack knew what he was doing, he was on his feet. His legs pumped. His arms swung, carrying him down the hill and straight into the heart of the battle. He wasn't watching it anymore. He was in it.

CHAPTER ONE

Riiiiiiiiinngggg!

The fourth-period bell rang, and Zack snapped back to attention. He and his best friend, Ollie Grossberg, spilled out into the crowded hallway, where everyone pushed and jostled to their next stop.

Zack looked down at his best friend as they headed toward the cafeteria. "Ollie, if you're going to keep falling asleep in class, you're going to have to start wearing a bib to school."

Ollie wiped at the dried drool on his cheek with the back of his hand. "How am I supposed to stay awake in World History? It's like she sprays sleeping potion into the air with her breath." Ollie stopped and pulled a small notebook from his back pocket. "Actually, a sprayable sleeping potion isn't a bad idea." He scribbled a few notes while they kept walking.

"Not that it matters," Zack said. "You could probably sleep through the whole thing and still get an A."

The two parked themselves at a corner table. Zack hunkered onto the little seat and pulled a large plastic container out of his knapsack. "Oh man," he said, "the only thing worse than microwave surprise is leftover microwave surprise." He pried open the lid and took a sniff. "All yours," he said, pushing it across to Ollie.

Between mouthfuls, Ollie said, "How can you hate your dad's cooking so much and still be eight feet tall?"

"Six-three," Zack corrected, grabbing half of Ollie's peanut butter and jelly sandwich. "And have you taken a look at my father or sister lately? Big kind of runs in the family." Zack reached into his pack again and pulled out his sketchpad. "Let me show you something." He flipped open the pad and pointed to a drawing. "I figure if we go ultra-lightweight, maybe an aluminum frame, we can get away with something really small to get the whole thing in the air, like maybe a modified hot air balloon. It can be blue or gray, something to camouflage against the sky. And then the camera mounts here."

"That frame is going to get in the way where it is," Ollie interrupted. He wiped away the wet crumbs that had just sprayed out of his mouth and onto the pad. "Sorry about that."

Zack started sketching. "What about like that? And maybe a three-hundred-sixty degree lens?"

"Good idea," garbled Ollie through another mouthful. "Good microwave surprise, too. What else have you got?"

"Just an orange."

"No, I mean, what's on that other page?"

Zack flipped the cover closed. "Nothing. Just something I was thinking about. Something to open a stuck locker. It's nothing, really."

"Stuck locker?" Ollie narrowed his eyes. "That's interesting. Now let me think. Isn't there someone we know who has a locker that's always sticking?"

Zack focused on peeling his orange. "I don't know. I guess so."

"Here's an idea," said Ollie. "Call me crazy, but what about *talking* to Ashley Williams? I mean, you can leave her all the mix CDs and open all the lockers you want, but I say the first step to meeting a girl is making sure she knows you're alive."

"She knows," Zack said. "Remember the last time I tried to talk to her? I fell off the back of the bleachers."

"Oh yeah. That was a brilliant move. Well guess what? Here comes your second chance."

Ollie pointed to where Ashley and three other girls were carrying their trays into the cafeteria. Zack looked over his shoulder, and his fingers clenched the orange he was holding so tightly that the skin broke. He kept his chin down and watched out of the corner of his eye as Ashley sat at a nearby table.

"Go on," Ollie whispered. "I dare you."

Zack wiped his hands on his sleeves, stalling and trying to think of something that wasn't too obvious.

Hi, Ashley.

Hey, Ashley, how's it going?

Hi, Ashley. I'm Zack.

Ugh.

Hi, Ashley. I'm Zack, the world's largest dork.

Splat!

A small pile of mashed potatoes landed on the floor at Zack's feet.

"Cream the freshmen!"

Across the cafeteria, sophomore bully Eric Spangler stood up on his seat. He leaned over, grabbed a handful of corn from the nearest freshman's tray, and mashed it in the kid's face. Eric's best friend and sidekick Doug Horner exploded with laughter, and so did several of their goons. They all started spreading out through the cafeteria like hyenas on the prowl. And experience showed that it was only a matter of time before Eric would hone in on Zack.

"Oh man, not again," Ollie groaned, as a pat of butter whizzed past his head. He raised his hand to his mouth and spoke into it like a walkie-talkie. "Gilman, come in Gilman. We have a positive I.D. on public enemy number one. Operation Pretty Girl is over. We're moving out. Do you copy?"

Zack stole another glance at Ashley as he packed up his things. Mostly, he was relieved. Even the back of her head made him nervous.

Then his stomach clenched as he saw Eric Spangler saunter over to Ashley, lean down, and whisper something in her ear. If there was one person who didn't deserve to be talking to Ashley Williams, it was Eric Spangler.

"Thanks," Zack heard Ashley say coolly. "But I don't need to be saved."

Excellent. Ashley Williams, one; Eric Spangler, zero.

As Zack and Ollie ducked out of the cafeteria door, a spoonful of fruit cocktail exploded against the wall like a wet grenade.

"Hey! Gutless Gilman! Gross Ollie!" Doug Horner's voice chased after them. "Where do you think you're going?"

Zack and Ollie kept walking without looking back. A moment later, they heard the unmistakable, booming voice of Mr. Ogmund, their principal. "Doug Horner. Put that piece of pizza down. Right now."

"Well at least they got nabbed this time," Ollie said.

Zack shrugged. "Doug Horner maybe. Not Eric Spangler."

Mrs. Spangler just happened to be school superintendent, as in, Mr. Ogmund's boss. It was no secret that Ogmund had a complete blind spot when it came to Eric.

"Spangler wears his mother like a bulletproof vest," Zack continued. "He'd pretty much have to blow up the school before he got into any trouble around here."

"He got in trouble for that fire," Ollie pointed out. "Like three months in the mini-slammer kind of trouble."

"Yeah," Zack said, feeling a familiar knot form in his stomach. "But that wasn't in school."

They stopped in front of their lockers. Zack stashed his sketchpad and grabbed a book for his next class.

"What an idiot," Ollie said. "I can't believe he tried to blame you for that fire. And I still can't believe you guys were ever friends."

Zack nodded, the knot tightening. "Yeah, well, that was a long time ago."

It was just as hard for *him* to believe he'd been friends with Eric as it was for Ollie. But he and Eric had grown up down the street from each other, and even though Eric was a year older, the two of them did everything together when they were kids. Then, as they got older, Eric started getting into some things that Zack wasn't okay with. Stupid stuff, like throwing rocks at neighbors' houses. Until one day, it was something bigger. They had ridden their bikes to an old abandoned warehouse. Eric wanted to break in. Zack didn't, and went home instead. It was the first time he'd ever stood up to Eric. It was also the first time Eric called him Gutless Gilman. Zack didn't even hear about the fire until the next day when Eric wasn't in school. The next time they saw each other was three months later when Eric came back from the detention center. Ever since then he had treated Zack like dog meat.

"Sorry, what did you say?" Zack looked over at Ollie, who was looking back at him expectantly.

"I said, Ogmund sucks up to Eric's mom like she's a tank of oxygen," Ollie said. Then he stopped in the middle of the hallway and made a vomiting sound. "Great, now I'm thinking about Ogmund and Mrs. Spangler."

Zack laughed. "Ogmund probably wishes he could marry her. Then he'd be Mrs. Spangler's lapdog *and* Eric's stepfather."

"Not that Eric cares. His father's like what? A zillionaire? Isn't he one of the owners of the Chicago Bears or something?"

"I know his dad lives in Chicago now," Zack said. "And I think he does something with the team. He's definitely got a lot of money."

"I just can't believe you guys were ever friends," Ollie said.

Zack stopped in the doorway of his next class, freshman English. "Yeah, you already said that. Thanks for reminding me."

"That's what friends are for."Ollie stood up on his toes, bringing the top of his head nearer to Zack's shoulder. "Anyway, you need any protection, you just let me know."

"Thanks," said Zack. "I'll keep it in mind."

❧

Walking home from school, Zack mentally worked on some of the details for Ashley's locker-opener.

Maybe a hand-held disk of some kind, with a free-turning handle. The handle works . . . what? An expanding arm, or a claw, something strong enough to hold up against metal.

He was more than a block from his house when he heard the familiar music. As he rounded the corner onto Lyman Avenue, he saw the Winnebago bouncing in his driveway and heard his father's off-tune singing.

Go Vikings, break through the line
Purple flying, all of the time
Go Vikings, run up the score
First down,
Touchdown,
Get us some more.
Go Vikings, never say no
V–I–K–I–N–G–S,
Go, Vikings, let's go!

Mrs. Tweedy stood scowling in her doorway as Zack passed her house. "Sorry, Mrs. Tweedy," he called out. Mrs. Tweedy pursed her lips at Zack and shut the door.

Zack kept his head down as he headed up the driveway. With a squeak from the shock absorbers, the big camper leaned toward Zack as if it were trying to get closer to him. The door flew open and Jock Gilman jumped out.

"The Zack's home!" he yelled, his palm in the air. His red beard, the same color as Zack's hair, was speckled with potato chip crumbs.

"Hey, Dad, Mrs. Tweedy was staring at me again. Could you maybe turn down the music?"

Jock stood with his hand still in the air. "Come on, don't leave me hanging here."

Zack reached up and gave his father a reluctant high five. Jock was one of the few people Zack knew who was taller than he was. Jock was also about twice as big around.

"We're going to have to work on Mrs. Tweedy," Jock said. He thumped himself on the chest of his XXL purple Minnesota sweatshirt. "That woman's got no Viking pride."

"That's true, Dad. But could you still turn it down?"

"Yeah, yeah, fine. But I think we're going to have to work on you, too. You're coming to the game on Sunday, aren't you?"

"I don't know." Zack started backing up toward the front door. "We'll see. Maybe."

"So it's set then," Jock called after him. "Good. Grab a case of soda from the kitchen and bring it out here. I'm stocking up the Winnie."

Zack wished his father hadn't named it the Winnie. Everyone thought the name was short for Winnebago, but it was actually after Zack's mom, Winnifred Gilman, who had died from pneumonia when Zack was five. Every time his father used the name, Zack was reminded of her, and of how normal life had seemed back then. Now they had a house that looked something like a football museum and an oversized camper for a family car. Zack wouldn't have minded a nice simple sedan or an SUV—anything that fit into one parking space and didn't have "Vikings Rule!" painted on the side in purple.

Zack made his way through the living room, past piles of magazines and newspapers, an unfinished Minnesota Vikings team photo jigsaw puzzle on the coffee table, and an out-stretched recliner that had broken in that position a year ago.

In the kitchen, his older sister, Valerie, was sitting with Hillary and Helena North. All three were looking at a piece of paper on the table.

"Dad wants a case of soda for the Winnie," Zack said.

"I got it last time," Valerie said without looking up.

"Yeah, fine, but where is it?"

"On the back porch."

Both of the North sisters looked up. "Hi, Zack," said one of them.

Zack looked at their identical faces, long blonde hair, and brilliant smiles. "Hi, uh . . ."

"Hillary," said Hillary.

Zack nodded and looked at the floor. Hillary and Helena

were probably the first and second most popular girls in the high school. He just didn't ever know which was which.

Helena held up a piece of paper. "Do you want to sign our petition? We're trying to get the school to have a girls' football team."

"Sure, I'll sign," Zack said. He pulled a purple Minnesota Vikings pen out of a Viking helmet pencil cup on the kitchen counter.

"You two might as well play football," Valerie said, stirring her iced tea. "You're already captains of everything else."

"Not the chess club," Hillary said.

"I was going to do chess this year but it meets at the same time as the mountain biking club," Helena said. "And next year, if we get football, I guess I'll have to ditch mountain biking, too."

"We'll see," Hillary said.

Zack signed his name under Valerie's and handed back the petition.

"You know, Zack," Helena said, "you should go out for football next year. You're like the biggest, tallest guy in school and you're only a freshman. I bet you'd be a natural."

"That's what I tell him all the time," said Jock. He stood in the doorway with a wrench in one hand and a dirty rag in the other.

"Hi, Mr. Gilman," both twins said in unison.

Jock put a meaty arm around Zack's neck while he spoke to the girls. "The Zack's a superstar waiting to happen. He's

13

just not a fighter; no fire in the belly. Isn't that right, Zack?"

Zack squirmed out from Jock's grip. He glared at his dad. "I'll get the soda."

From the back porch, Zack heard one of the twins' voices.

"So what do you think, Mr. Gilman? Feeling lucky?"

"Now girls," Jock answered, "I don't want to embarrass you again."

"So you're scared, is that it?"

Zack heard the scraping of kitchen chairs across the floor. He grabbed a case of soda and hurried back into the room. Hillary and Helena were sitting across from Jock, each with an elbow on the table. Jock leaned in and grasped the twins' hands with one palm, ready to arm wrestle.

"Valerie, you want in on this?" Jock asked. "Three against one?"

Valerie leaned against the sink, watching. "With those greasy hands of yours? No thanks. Hillary and Helena can take care of themselves."

The twins didn't respond. They were both staring intently at Jock, waiting for the signal.

"All right then. Count off."

Valerie stepped closer. "One. Two. Three!"

It took about a minute and a half. Zack and Valerie cheered on the North sisters. First Hillary and Helena's faces turned red, then Jock's. Their arms wavered but all three hands stayed upright. Then slowly, slowly, Jock pushed them away, finally pinning the backs of both their hands to the top of the kitchen table.

Jock stood up and held his hands over his head in two fists, jumping around the kitchen.

"Lucky break, Mr. Gilman," Hillary said, smiling and rubbing her fingers.

Jock chuckled. He pointed to the picture of a Minnesota Vikings helmet on his sweatshirt and thumped his chest. "More than luck girls. It's Purple Pride. But thanks for letting the old man look good in front of his kids."

Zack and Valerie both rolled their eyes. Each of the twins high-fived Jock in turn.

"Are you going to the game this weekend?" Hillary asked.

"Never miss a game," Jock said proudly. He opened the refrigerator and peered inside.

"That's only partly true," Valerie said. "He goes to the parking lot and listens to the game on the radio with his friends."

"Now that is dedication," said a twin.

"See that?" Jock said. "Dedication." He pulled out a plastic container, sniffed whatever was inside, and turned down the corners of his mouth. "I think this one's older than you are, Zack." He closed the container and put it back in the refrigerator. "Anyway, maybe we'll see you at the stadium. The Zack's coming, too."

"Hello?" Valerie said, waving her hands. "Ever think about inviting me?"

"Sorry about that, Val, figured you weren't interested," Jock said. "So, Zack and Valerie are coming, too."

"No, I'm not," said Valerie. "I just thought it would be nice to be asked. For once."

Jock shrugged and laughed good-naturedly. "Anyway, Zack's coming."

"No, I'm not," Zack said.

"Sure you are," said Jock. He pulled out another plastic container and again sniffed whatever was inside. "Dinner's ready!" he pronounced after the contents apparently passed the test.

"I'm not going to the game," Zack repeated. "I have stuff to do."

"We'll see," Jock said.

Zack didn't know why he bothered arguing with his father anymore. Trying to win an argument with Jock Gilman was like trying to shove an elephant through a revolving door—it just wasn't going to happen. Zack knew that no matter what he said, he'd be in the Winnie Sunday afternoon, heading out to the Metrodome.

Zack took a look at the glop his father was spooning onto plates, and escaped to his room. He closed the door behind him and flipped on the high-intensity lighting over his workbench. The bench was just an old piece of kitchen counter with two-by-four planks for legs but it worked well enough for Zack. One of the advantages of having a father like Jock was getting to keep his room however he wanted. The workbench was littered with old sketches and half-finished models. Some tools hung on the wall, others were scattered around the room. A four-foot-high prototype for a telescope-style expandable climbing tower stood in one corner. It was draped with almost everything Zack had worn in the last week.

The one neat space in the room was Zack's bedside table, where a framed photo of his mother stood. Zack kept the picture facing away from his workbench. She probably would have hated the mess.

He sat down, cleared a space, and pulled out his sketchpad. The locker gadget seemed like a simple idea but so far he hadn't been able to come up with a way to build it that could actually work.

And so much for making any progress by Monday.

Now he was going to spend half his weekend in the Winnie, hanging out in the Metrodome parking lot. Just him and his father. And about three thousand pounds of his father's friends.

Great.

CHAPTER TWO

Purple Pride is coming through
Coming to town and
Coming to get you!
Purple Pride is the way of the game
Of glory, of fame,
The Viking name!

Jock sang loudly as he steered the Winnie onto the highway. He turned to Zack. "You fired up, Gilman? You seem kind of quiet."

Zack was watching the steel gray sky through the windshield. He faced his father, taking in Jock's plastic Viking helmet with the long blonde braids that hung down on either side of his head. "You know, Dad," he said, "I'm pretty sure real Viking helmets didn't come with their own hair."

"No changing the subject," Jock barked. "Are you *fired up*?!"

"Yeah sure," Zack said, trying to sound enthusiastic. "The Vikings are going to kick some Bear butt."

Jock laughed. "You said 'bare butt.'"

Zack rolled his eyes.

"Okay," Jock continued. "Pop quiz. Vikings are on the

twenty, third down and twelve. Score's eleven to eight, Bears. Thirty seconds on the clock. What do you do?"

Zack grabbed his father's homemade playbook off the dashboard. Jock had invented dozens of plays and strategies. Each one was carefully mapped in an old dog-eared journal. Zack quickly flipped through its pages while Jock *tick-tick-tick*ed like a clock.

"Ummmm. Maybe run a Gopher Push?"

Jock made a buzzer sound. "Sorry, nice try. With the Bears' defense, all you're going to get from a Gopher Push is a mouthful of Astroturf. Try again."

Zack tried to think, but it seemed like his brain was football-proof. Nothing stuck. Everything Jock ever told him just bounced right off.

"I don't know," he said. "Tic-Tackle-Toe?"

"I don't think so," Jock said. "Not with thirty seconds on the clock. You have to take everything into account, and you have to work fast. I'm thinking the Gilman Fake. Fake it up the middle, and then run it outside."

Zack smacked his forehead. "I should have guessed that." The Gilman Fake was by far Jock's favorite play.

"Not guessed," Jock said. "You don't win by guessing. You've got to know the plays."

Zack nodded. It was easier than saying what he was thinking. *Not going to happen. I'm not you.*

He knew he would probably never be like his father. He just wasn't sure that was such a bad thing.

When they pulled into the Metrodome parking lot, most of Jock's gang was already there. Larry Teegarden

19

jumped up and high-fived the windshield, leaving behind a smudged handprint. Smitty, Harlan, and Swan were still passing around the body paint and turning one another purple.

"Come on out and say hi to the guys," Jock said.

"It's cold out," said Zack. "I'm just going to hang out in the back of the Winnie, okay?"

"Sure thing," Jock said. "I'll just invite them all in instead."

That was all Zack needed to hear. He turned and followed his father outside. Immediately, the faces of all the guys lit up.

"Hey, it's the Zack!" Harlan called.

"Hey, guys," Zack said. Harlan held out a tube of body paint but Zack held up his hand to decline.

Larry came running over to them. "Zackaroni! What's up? And where's the—"

"Chips?" finished Zack. He pointed to the Winnie. "They're on the table."

"Great. How about the—"

"Soda's under the sink."

Larry slapped Zack on the back, shook hands with Jock and disappeared into the Winnie. He came out a moment later with several drinks in his hands and a bag of chips under each arm.

"All right, big Jock and little Jock are here," said Swan Swanson, Jock's best friend. "Let the tailgate begin." His shirt was off and he had a purple "V" across his chest. His face was painted bright gold, with purple circles around the eyes. When he walked over to greet them, he was obviously favoring his right leg.

"How's the knee, Swan?" Jock took a tube of paint from him and started slathering his own face.

"I can still crack some skulls," Swan said. "Kind of like that time, remember? In Manitoba? There must have been eighteen other guys chasing after us. . . ."

Zack had heard the Manitoba story several times. Last time Swan told it, there had been twelve guys chasing after them. As he continued talking, Zack started thinking about how warm it must be inside the Winnie. Jock stripped off his T-shirt and started making a big "M" to match the "V" on Swan's torso. Zack shivered just looking at him. He zipped his army jacket all the way up.

"Aren't you guys cold?" he asked. "It's going to snow, you know."

"Anything for the team!" Harlan shouted. He raised a fist and charged. The whole gang ran toward Zack at once and crashed together in a spontaneous group belly bump. Zack jumped out of the way just in time, while Harlan, Larry, Smitty, Swan, and Jock went bouncing off in different directions, hooting like insane square dancers.

Zack started inching his way toward the Winnie's door. Maybe he could slip away unnoticed.

Carl Smith—Smitty to everyone else—popped his trunk and tossed out a purple-and-gold foam football. He opened his driver's-side door and cranked up the stereo. Most of the guys sang along.

". . . V–I–K–I–N–G–S,
Go, Vikings, let's go!"

Swan took a pass from Jock and tossed the foam ball over to Smitty. "Hey, Smitty, how come you never sing?"

Smitty shrugged and passed the ball to Larry. Zack put a hand on the Winnie's doorknob. Two more steps and he was clear.

"Same reason Smitty never says anything," Larry yelled.

"Hey, Swan," Harlan called out, "how come you always ask the same questions?"

"I don't know," said Swan. "I figure maybe someday he'll actually answer me."

Smitty nodded.

"See that? Maybe he will. Someday. Hey, Zack, catch!"

Zack was just about to step inside. He turned and reached too late. The ball bounced off his fingertips and landed at his feet.

"A little help?" Jock called, waving. "Right here, Zack, perfect spiral."

Zack looked at the ball. He picked it up and threw. The ball sailed into the air, past Jock, over several rows of cars, and disappeared somewhere in the parking lot.

"See that?" said Jock. "He's a natural. Doesn't even know his own strength. Oh, and Zack, buddy? We're going to miss you. But come back soon."

Zack knew the rules of the game well enough. Last one to touch the ball has to go get it. He walked with his eyes on the ground. Most likely it had rolled under a car and he'd never find it. The parking lot was a maze of people, cars, vans, and trucks. Vendors were everywhere, selling Viking programs, banners, clothing, balls, cups, spare tire covers. . . .

Zack's mind wandered as he walked. He thought about what his father had just said. If there was one thing Zack didn't feel like, it was a natural football player.

Two left feet. No interest in the game. Yeah, I'm a perfect candidate. Right.

Zack imagined Jock would weep with joy if he even showed a little interest in going out for the school team. Then he imagined Jock and his friends at the games, painted up and shouting like banshees in the stands. Just the idea of it made him shudder. At least here, his father was one of thousands of other superfans. If there was a single place in the world Jock Gilman could blend in, it was the Metrodome parking lot before a game.

"Looking for this?"

Zack raised his eyes from the concrete. The good news was that he had found the ball. The bad news was that the ball was sitting in Eric Spangler's hands.

Spangler, Doug Horner, and their usual gang of goons were all decked out in Chicago Bears gear, no doubt the latest care package sent up from Chicago by Eric's father. They all looked like miniature versions of Jock's gang, but with navy blue and orange faces instead of purple and gold.

"Hello? Anyone there?" Eric said, waving the ball in front of Zack's face.

Zack took a deep breath. "Come on, Spangler, give it a rest."

"Come on, Spangler," said one of the guys in a high-pitched whiny voice, "give it a rest."

Zack's heart started beating faster but he kept his face still, no emotion. "Just give me the ball, okay?"

"You want it back?" Eric taunted, holding out the ball. "That's cool. It's just a piece of Viking garbage anyway. Here you go."

Zack reached for the ball and Eric tossed it back over his shoulder to Horner. Horner caught it, and then hauled off and threw it back the way Zack had come. As the ball left Horner's hand, Zack heard a dull *pop*, followed by a groan.

Horner looked down at his throwing arm, which now hung limply at his side. "Oh, man. Did you guys see 'Wrestle Fat City' last night? This is just what happened to the Sledge." His shoulder looked like it had been twisted permanently forward. Several of the other guys started laughing.

Spangler turned to look at Horner. "Again?"

Horner rubbed his shoulder and winced. "I don't get it, man. It just pops out like that—" He snapped his fingers and immediately doubled over with another groan. "No. More. Snapping. Fingers."

"You are such an idiot," Eric said, and then turned his attention back to Zack. "So it looks like you lost your ball again. What are you going to do about it?"

Zack stared back at Eric, almost wishing he was the kind of guy to just start swinging. "You know, Eric, whatever happened between you and me was when I was in fifth grade. You were in sixth. Remember? Sixth grade. Are you going to hold onto that the rest of your life?"

Eric stepped closer. "Are you going to keep walking away the rest of your life?"

His goons stepped closer, too, Doug Horner cradling his arm but still eyeing Zack menacingly. Zack stood his ground, but he felt as though his heart were beating somewhere between his throat and his tongue.

Just be calm, Gilman. Just turn and go.

Eric stuck his chin in the air and looked up at Zack. "You know, I'm curious about something. You're like, what? Six foot eight? Twelve hundred pounds? What are you so afraid of?"

"Clothesline him, Eric!" Horner shouted. "Piledrive him onto the concrete. Do it, man!"

Now Zack and Eric both broke their stare and looked over at Horner until he shut up.

"Where were we?" Eric said.

"I was just leaving," said Zack. He turned and walked away, breathing slowly through his nose, trying to keep calm.

Eric called after him. "Oh yeah, that's right, that's what you do. Go back to your daddy. You always were a wuss."

Zack could hear the guys laughing. He tried to block it out, along with the persistent, nagging voice in the back of his head.

Maybe it's true. Maybe I am just a wimp.

He clenched his fists at his sides and kept walking. Before he was out of earshot, he heard one more shout from Eric.

"Vikings suck!"

When he got back to the Winnie, Jock held up the foam football. "Good pass," he said. "You got it right back to us."

25

"Thanks," Zack said quietly. "I'm just going to go inside." He made his way to the back of the Winnie and lay down on the bench seat. A Vikings cheerleader smiled down at him from a poster taped to the ceiling. Zack couldn't shake the feeling that it looked like she was laughing at him.

He closed his eyes and tried to push his thoughts somewhere else. Slowly, he focused in on his workbench at home. He imagined his sketch pad. He mentally opened it to a new page and started making plans.

Spring-loaded, portable catapult. Swivel head action. Fully transformable, with a payload for hurling large objects, or a crusher bar for catching anything that tripped the lock mechanism. Crusher bar essentially works on a mousetrap principle—spring loaded to flip one hundred-eighty degrees. Strong enough to crush a high school sophomore.

Zack's thoughts were invaded by a pounding on the back window. He opened his eyes. The Minnesota Vikings curtains bounced with each slam.

"Need! Food! Need! Food! Need! Food!" Zack heard Larry chanting. The other guys quickly took it up.

"Need! Food! Need! Food! Need! Food!"

A cold blast of air filled the Winnie as the door opened and Jock stepped inside. The tip of his plastic helmet scraped against the ceiling.

"Hey, guess what?" said Jock. "You've been elected vice president in charge of bratwurst. Congratulations. We'll take twelve, all onions, ten with mustard."

Zack sat up. "I just got back." He could tell how this was

26

going to go, but he persisted anyway. "I'll flip you for it." He fished into his pocket for a quarter, but it was too late.

Jock leaned his head out the door. "Hey! He doesn't want to go."

Before Zack could do anything, Larry, Harlan, Smitty, and Swan all piled in and the Winnie was wall-to-wall with purple-painted superfans. Zack had never been inside one of those little cars at the circus, the kind where twenty clowns come pouring out, but now he could imagine what it must be like.

The guys took up a new chant, "Zack! Zack! Zack! Zack!" and bounced the Winnie up and down mercilessly.

Zack tried not to laugh. He knew it only encouraged them. The noise was tremendous, punching Zack's cardrums over and over. Smitty got an arm around Zack's shoulders and squeezed his neck in a half-Nelson while they kept chanting.

Zack wrestled himself free. "Who's the kid here, anyway?"

Larry and Harlan raised their hands, shouting "I am! I am!" which cracked everyone up even more. The longer Zack stalled, the wilder it got. Any minute now they were going to start belly bumping inside the Winnie, and Zack did not want to be around to see that, much less get caught in the middle.

"All right, all right, fine!" He held out his hand and a few of the guys pulled wrinkled bills out of their pockets as he squeezed his way toward the door. The "Zack, Zack, Zack" chant now turned to "Brat-wurst, brat-wurst, brat-wurst!"

When Zack stepped outside, a light snow was beginning to fall. He turned up his collar and started walking. Most people loved the first snow of the year. To Zack, it was a reminder of how much he couldn't wait to live somewhere else. California, maybe, or Florida. Better yet, Mexico. They didn't have football in Mexico.

Jock leaned his head out and called after him. "Remember . . ."

"I know," said Zack, "Twelve with onions, two no mustard."

"Plus whatever you want. That's my boy! Love you, son!"

Zack waved over his shoulder and kept going. Normally, he would have headed right toward the stadium for the brat wagon, but that would mean going back toward Spangler and Horner. He mentally navigated the long way around, and headed in that direction.

The flat gray sky hadn't given any clues that morning what it was going to do, even though the weather reports had predicted snow. Minnesota winters were famous for their intensity—snow squalls and sixty-below-zero temperatures and house-swallowing drifts. Some years, it was mid-January before it got bad; other years, there was skiing in October. Either way, it always stretched into what were supposed to be the spring months. The year Zack's mom died, it had snowed on Mother's Day.

Almost immediately it started snowing harder, the kind of big wet flakes that melt right away but act like messengers of more to come. Zack ran a hand through his wet hair and looked around for the bratwurst wagon.

Among the hundreds of people, his eyes fell on one family in particular. The back of their Mercedes wagon was up, and the mom was pouring something hot from a thermos into mugs. The dad, son, and daughter were tossing a ball around. The son said something and everyone laughed. They looked like something out of a car commercial, and for just a second, Zack imagined himself tossing that football and drinking something hot out of that thermos.

All over the parking lot, the scene was quickly disintegrating. Like a television losing its picture, snow started to fill the air, erasing Zack's view. He couldn't see more than a few cars in any direction. The snow was starting to drift and the wind was picking up as well. A storm was coming on fast.

Zack realized with a sudden jolt that he hadn't paid attention to where he was going. The snow was so dense now he couldn't even see the stadium. Even if he had taken his usual route to the brat wagon, it would have been hard to get back to the Winnie. As he looked around, Zack fought off an edge of panic. Never mind the Winnie at this point—where was *anything*?

In outer space, he had heard, there was no such thing as direction—no up, no down, no east or west. Now it was easy to imagine what that must be like. Other than having his feet on the ground, Zack couldn't see the parking lot, the sky, or anything distinguishable on any side. It was all just a swirl of blowing snow. On top of it all, he felt as though the temperature had dropped at least twenty degrees and was still going down. If he was going to get anywhere, he needed to move. He tucked his chin, picked a direction, and started walking.

Zack tried not to think too much. If he didn't think, he wouldn't panic.

Take a step. Take a step. Take a step.

There was nothing else he could do. The wind stung his eyes and face. All he could see was blowing snow. It was like traveling inside a white ball.

Suddenly, something caught his eye. A dark figure darted across his field of vision. It was hard to tell how far away it was, or even if it was a person. Zack didn't care. He ran after it.

"Hey!" he yelled. "Wait up!" He could barely hear his own voice above the wind. He had only caught a glimpse of whoever—or whatever—it had been, but he kept running. His boot struck something in the snow, and he went down hard. A shock of pain broke through the cold as his head and hands scraped the rough concrete. He rolled onto his back and pounded the ground with his fist. He touched his forehead. At least there was no blood.

Zack eased himself up. Whatever he had tripped on was sticking out of the snow. He picked it up and looked at it. It was heavy, some kind of metal object. Someone must have dropped it.

It might have been made out of iron. Whatever it was, it was too rusty and dirty to tell. It looked as if it had been buried for a long time. So what was it doing here in the snow?

The strange object was round, like a miniature hubcap, but with three arms or stems sticking out and dividing the circle into thirds. The center of the circle was a carving that looked like a cloud or a flower of some kind, with branches twisting away in every direction. Each branch wound around itself and the others in a complex pattern, like a twisted maze of garden hose. And each of those ended in one of the three stems, the thickness of Zack's finger, with some kind of differently shaped tab on the end.

Zack stared at the object in his hand. Nothing about it made sense but it was the only thing besides blowing whiteness he could see. He held tightly to it. Then, through his nearly numb fingers, it started to feel warm. Zack didn't care if his mind was playing tricks on him or not. The relief was intense.

He hugged the thing against his chest as it started to heat up. A soft warmth spread through his body. At the same time, the storm got even fiercer. The wind screamed now. The snow clawed like fingernails on his face. Zack doubled over, trying to focus only on the heat of the object in his hands. As it got warmer, the storm got worse. And then all at once, like an explosion, the thing was too hot to keep hold of. The storm seemed to blow itself out in one last mighty gust. Zack stumbled to the side and accidentally dropped the object to the ground.

The sudden silence was eerie. A light snow was gently falling, nothing compared to just a few seconds ago. Zack's thoughts seemed to echo loudly inside his head.

What just happened?

When he picked up the object again, it was cold. It had also completely changed. Any sign of rust or dirt was gone. The strange thing was now a burnished silver, the color of a nickel. It looked brand new. Zack wondered if he was starting to lose his mind. And then he looked around.

Too late. I've already lost it.

He was in the middle of a completely unfamiliar wilderness. The stadium was nowhere to be seen, much less the parking lot, the Winnie, or a single person. As far as Zack could see, he was completely alone.

On one side of him, Zack saw a range of snow-covered hills receding into the distance. On the other side was an expanse of rocky ground. The snow cover was broken only by a few trees, which looked as gnarled and weather-beaten as Zack felt. He turned around and saw a water line far behind him at the horizon.

Not only was he not at the Metrodome, he didn't seem to be in Minneapolis, or even Minnesota anymore.

Zack turned, staring blankly in each direction. He had no idea how long it had been since he left his father in the parking lot. Two hours? Fifteen minutes? Or maybe he was still there. Maybe he was lying facedown in the snow, out cold where he had fallen. Just like Dorothy in that tornado on the way to Oz. This had to be some kind of dream. Either that, or he had checked into Hotel Crazy for a nice long stay.

Zack shook his head. He jumped up and down. He yelled out loud. "Wake up!" None of it seemed to have any effect. He had never felt stuck in a dream before. Usually, he just woke up in the morning or when the dream was over.

Well, as long as I'm dreaming, at least I'm not dead. I guess.

Zack did the only thing he could think to do. He started walking.

One thing was still the same as before. It was still freezing cold. Zack pulled his hands up into his sleeves and carried the mystery object under one arm, hoping it would crank out some more heat.

He tried to imagine the sun coming out. Maybe he could take control of this dream, at least make it more comfortable. While he was at it, he imagined an extra large meatball and double cheese pizza. But none of it worked. Everything stayed the same.

He trudged along, keeping his eyes peeled for any sign of life. As far as he could tell, it was just miles of nothing. Cold air scorched his lungs as he huffed up a short, steep hill. His feet ached. His stomach started to growl.

Graargh.

At least, he thought it was his stomach. He stopped and listened. There it was again, another growl, louder this time. And behind him.

Graaaargghhh!

Zack turned around. The charging mob was about fifty feet away and bearing down on him like a bullet train.

Zack had become so accustomed to seeing nothing but snow that the image of four dozen sword-carrying warriors in full battle gear was like an electric shock to his brain. He stood frozen, staring, too stunned to move.

The mob closed in.

GRAAAARGGHHH!

Twenty feet.

Ten feet.

Five feet.

Move, Gilman. MOVE!

Zack dove out of the way just in time.

CHAPTER THREE

The mob flew past Zack. Before he had even finished spitting out the snow lodged in his mouth, they had disappeared over the crest of the hill.

Zack searched the swirl of confusion in his head and tried to pick out some of the details of what had just happened. A few of the warriors had actually looked at him as they charged past, but the group seemed to travel with one will.

Most of them had been wearing pointed metal helmets with face shields that covered their eyes and noses. The tallest one had been swinging a double-edged axe over his head. Most of them had looked at least as big as Zack. Definitely not a group to mess with. Their yells and growls alone were nearly overwhelming. For a moment as they passed by, it had been as loud in the open air as it had been back inside the Winnie with all of his father's gang. Now the Winnie was exactly where Zack wished he could be. At least the Winnie was warm—and safe.

Another roar of voices came from somewhere beyond the crest of the hill. This one sounded like an even larger group than the one Zack had already seen. Keeping low to the ground, he crept forward. Spread out in the field below him, he saw that the original mob had joined forces with another group. They all had the same sort of old-style battle gear. Some were clearly archers, with quivers of arrows strapped to their backs. Most carried the same sort of round shield, and almost everyone had some kind of sword. Near the center of their line, a pole with a banner had been planted in the ground. The banner had a yellow-and-white diamond pattern and flapped gently in the light wind.

The tribe on the other side of the field was even more puzzling. They looked more animal-like, in their dark fur cloaks and hoods. They pawed at the ground with their feet and shook their heads from side to side like dogs tearing at raw meat.

The one thing both sides had in common was that they were heavily armed.

A slow drumming began. Zack looked back to the near side and saw the biggest guy of the group, beating on the side of his shield with his sword. He was a huge warrior and seemed to be some kind of leader. When he turned his head, Zack saw the man's red beard, pulled into a short braid that hung from his chin. Everything above his mouth was masked by the steel of his helmet. Soon, the others around him took up the pounding of swords against shields. It spread down the line until all of them were beating in unison.

Something about the rhythm jarred a memory in Zack's head. A blip that he didn't even know he had held onto. It was something Mrs. Watson, his World History teacher, had said. He could just hear her voice now.

"*. . . the Vikings of ninth-century Scandinavia . . .*"

That was it. Vikings. Of course.

It made perfect sense that he would be dreaming about Vikings. This was some sort of weird football-inspired dream that his father was going to love hearing about.

The beating picked up, a little faster now. Zack heard a few low voices rumbling. As the drumming accelerated, the voices grew. The thumping sound was ordered and rhythmic, even as it sped up.

On the other side of the field, the group with the hoods and fur cloaks became even more agitated. Their growls became roars and shouts and strangely pitched moans, a contrast to the evenly paced drumming on the near side. They began violently shoving each other, as if they couldn't wait to fight and were starting in on one another.

The red-bearded leader on the near side raised his sword in the air and yelled something to the group. A score of archers reached back to their quivers, loaded their bows, and fired a volley of arrows over the heads on the other side and into the woods beyond. It must have been some kind of pre-battle custom. It was quickly followed by another bellow from the leader, and the battle was on.

Zack watched with fascinated horror as the two sides rushed toward each other. They met in the middle of the field with an immediate metallic clashing of swords. Soon the battle was spread out into dozens of skirmishes, more than Zack could look at all at once. He winced, sucking in short gasps of air every time he saw someone take a blow. It seemed as real as any movie—or dream—he had ever experienced. One fighter backed another man up against a tree as they covered ground, crossing swords. He faked a swing one way and then countered in the other direction, then seemed to drive his sword right through the man and into the tree itself. The man went limp and then fell to the ground when the sword was withdrawn.

Zack took a deep breath. He couldn't ignore the question that was starting to gnaw at him.

What happens if you die in a dream? Is that it?

Dream or no dream, his head was starting to swim.

And then he saw something that topped it all. Something that pulled him off the sidelines and right into the battle itself.

Directly below Zack at the bottom of the hill, the red-bearded leader and another soldier were surrounded by fur-cloaked opponents. One enemy fighter stepped in and swung his hammer. The red-bearded man caught it fully in the chest. He staggered to the side. As he fell to one knee, his helmet slipped off. For the first time, Zack saw the man's face.

No way. Not possible. Error.

It was Jock Gilman's face. His father's face.

Zack put both hands on top of his head as if to keep the thoughts from exploding out of his own skull. Jock Gilman, the man he knew as his father, the man who thought of channel surfing as "working out," was down there fighting, swinging a sword, and *kicking butt*. That sight alone was stranger than everything else Zack had seen put together. And just behind the amazement and the disbelief came a rush of adrenaline. Jock was struggling back to his feet. His opponent held a sword high up in the air.

That's when Zack charged.

Before he knew what he was doing, he was hurtling down the hill toward his father. Whatever propelled him, it didn't come as words or thoughts. Instinct carried him forward. His legs pumped. His vision closed in around Jock, shutting out everything else.

Another fraction of a second and Zack would have been too late. Jock gripped the handle of his axe. The other fighter swung his sword. Zack barreled into the fray.

He realized too late that he couldn't stop if he wanted to. Momentum carried him straight into the fighting circle like a giant bowling ball, taking down warriors like pins as he went. He crashed into his father and they rolled, one over the other.

Zack lay on his back, gasping for air, the wind knocked out of him.

Another enemy soldier suddenly leapt forward. He was short and hunched, with pointed yellow teeth. Instead of a fur cloak, he seemed to be actually covered with dark furlike skin. Whatever he was, it wasn't human—more like some kind of ogre. If Zack had even a second to react, he might have screamed, but everything happened in a flash.

The ogre-creature went straight for the carved metal object Zack still held in his hand. Zack instinctively tightened his grip. The creature grabbed it and pulled.

A shock of electricity shot up Zack's arm. It looked as if the same thing was happening even more strongly on the other end. The creature's eyes bugged wide open. His teeth seemed to clench involuntarily. His hand shook and the tremor quickly moved up his arm to his shoulder, neck, and head. With a sudden explosive force, the creature flew backward through the air, as if he had been shot out of a cannon. Zack went rolling in the other direction.

Everyone started pushing and shouting. Zack looked at the mysterious object in his hand. The last thing he wanted now was another shock like the one he had just received. He dropped the thing and sat up quickly.

Jock and another of his men immediately stepped in and shielded Zack while everyone clamored to get closer. They all shouted and hissed but none of the words were familiar.

"Dad?" said Zack weakly. It was all he could think to say.

Jock babbled over his shoulder at Zack in the same strange language as the others. He pointed furiously to the thing on the ground. He seemed to be telling Zack to pick it up again. Zack was too stunned to do anything but obey. He slowly reached over, closed his eyes, grit his teeth, and grabbed onto it.

"He is here!"

"It has happened!"

His eyes were still closed when he realized that he could understand what they were saying. Somehow, the language was the same as before but the words were now clear to him.

"Get back!"

"Blasted cowards!"

Jock hauled Zack to his feet. He grabbed Zack's wrist and

waved the thing in the air. The enemy soldiers seemed to keep their distance now. Several of them began to slowly back away. Jock waved Zack's arm like a flag.

"Tell your prince that a new day has come!"

The soldiers with the furs and hoods continued backing up. Several of them turned and ran back toward the woods. Within a few minutes, they had cleared the field. Everyone who was left let up a huge cheer.

Just a dream. Just a dream. Go with it. At least they seem happy to see me.

Everything seemed so real, though, Zack had a hard time speaking. Jock was looking at him, eyes shining.

"Dad? What's . . . going on?"

The words were English in his brain, but something else was coming out of his mouth. He was speaking in their language.

"Hail the Lost Boy," Jock called, going down on one knee.

"Hail the Lost Boy," repeated all the others, removing their helmets and kneeling as well.

"Hail Yggdrasil's Key," called Jock, raising his sword.

"Hail Yggdrasil's Key," they repeated.

EGG–drah–zil? It wasn't a word Zack recognized. But they also said "key." Was that what he was carrying? A key?

Zack scanned the group. Amongst the dirty blood-smeared faces, several familiar figures jumped out at him. Harlan was there, right next to Smitty and Larry. They all had beards but it was definitely them. Deeper in the crowd, Zack saw that many of the soldiers were women. And perhaps strangest of all, amongst them were Hillary and Helena

North. The twins held battered silver helmets at their sides and wore long chain-mail coats that hung to the ground. Like everyone else, they looked solemnly at Zack as if they were seeing him for the first time.

Zack looked at the ground to hide his smile. Everyone was so serious, but this dream was almost funny now.

Jock rose to his feet and spoke again. "Lost Boy," he said. "Will you do us the honor of traveling to our humble village?" He bowed his head, waiting for an answer.

"Lost Boy?" said Zack. "It's me. Zack."

Jock looked up but said nothing. Zack put a hand to his chest. "Zack," he said again, louder. "Zack."

He heard several in the group quietly repeat it amongst themselves. "Zack, Zack, Zack." For a second it felt as though he were training parrots.

"Zack," said Jock, "will you do us the honor of traveling to our humble village?"

Zack shrugged. "Uh, sure." There didn't seem to be anything else to say, and there was no way he was going to stay out here alone.

Jock stood and engulfed Zack in a bear hug. Zack noticed the body odor even more than the feeling of being crushed by Jock's huge arms. The smell hit him like an onion-stuffed sweat sock. He tried to breathe through his mouth and keep his nose closed. Apparently, even smells felt real in this dream.

Everyone else crowded in, jostling Zack and slapping him on the back.

"I am Jok," Jock said, pronouncing it *joke*. "I am chieftain of this tribe. We thank you for appearing to us, by the power of Thor."

Zack recognized the name Thor from comics. He also knew Thor was a Viking god of some kind.

So I was right. They are supposed to be Vikings.

Jok motioned for the North twins to come over and introduced them as Hilda and Helga.

"No, I'm Helga," said one. "This is Hilda." Each of them in turn grasped Zack's hand and forearm in a bone-crunching shake. Zack wondered if Hilda was Hillary and Helga was Helena, or the other way around. Either way, it seemed that together they were the leaders of a second tribe.

"So are you guys all on one . . . team?" Zack asked.

"We are two tribes," Hilda said, "with one enemy."

"The Bears of the North," said Helga.

The name made perfect sense. Zack realized that the furs and hoods on the other soldiers had looked a lot like bearskin rugs. As soon as Helga said the name "Bears," everyone around them grew very serious.

"We should go," said one of the men.

"Harald is right," Jok said. He called for everyone to move out.

Several of the soldiers limped along with slashes on their arms and legs, but everyone walked without help. Many of them held handfuls of snow against their wounds. Despite any injuries, the tribes kept a brisk pace across the snowy ground. Zack was quickly out of breath.

For the first time in hours, he started to feel warm.

He trotted alongside Harald, the man he knew from home as Harlan.

"We are glad you will be traveling with us, Lost Boy," Harald said. The scratchy voice was the same. Everything about him was the same. He looked Zack up and down. "You wear interesting trousers," he said. "And your cloak—I've never seen one like it."

Zack glanced down at his jeans and green army jacket. *I guess my clothes look as weird to them as theirs do to me*, he realized. *Or weirder—since at least I've seen theirs in books!*

Zack held up the object he still carried with him, too big for any of his pockets. "You guys called this some kind of key, didn't you?"

"Yggdrasil's Key," said Harald. "Surely you know this already."

"Nope," Zack said. "I don't. Does it open a door, or . . . three doors, or something?" The key's three stems were each shaped differently. "Or something with three locks?"

Harald seemed to be avoiding Zack's glance. He motioned to Jok and a few of the others. Jok came over, followed by the men Zack knew as Larry and Smitty.

The one who looked like Larry, tall and thin with stringy brown hair, carried the tribe's yellow and white banner over his shoulder. He looked like a human flagpole.

"I am Lars," he said, "and this is Sigurd."

Sigurd silently nodded to Zack.

"The Lost Boy is asking about Yggdrasil's Key. He

doesn't seem to . . ." Harald trailed off.

"What do you know about it?" Jok asked gently.

"Well," Zack said, "I think it's why I'm here. Maybe it brought me here somehow?"

"Yes!" cried Jok. "So you know about the prophecy!"

Harald exhaled loudly and looked at Zack.

"Prophecy?" Zack asked.

The same shadow crossed all of the men's faces at once.

Jok spoke in low tones. "We will wait until we are back to the village. Keep the key with you. Always. Do you understand?"

"I think so," Zack said, although now he had more questions than ever.

"Always," Jok repeated sternly.

After a lengthy hike, they arrived at the shoreline where two similar ships were beached. Each of them was long, shallow, and tapered at the ends. Zack noticed they were shaped like stretched-out footballs. Their hulls were made from overlapping wooden planks and each had a tall mast with a sail. The sails were lowered and lashed to a cross-beam at the bottom of the mast.

The pointed front ends of each ship curved upward in a tall, intricately carved stem. At the top of one, the wood had been carved into a spiral shape, like a curled-up octopus tentacle. The other ship was topped by a dragon's head with its open mouth and rows of pointed teeth cast into a fierce expression.

Someone was waiting aboard the dragon ship. Jok held

up an open palm to the man. He let out an animal-like growl. "Aughhhhhh!"

The heavy-set silver-haired man on board returned the yell. He shook a wooden walking stick in the air. Suddenly Zack realized who had been missing. He had seen all his father's friends except Swan Swanson.

The man stopped short when he saw Zack. As the tribe drew closer, he shouted out to them.

"Has it happened?"

Several of the tribe shouted back their affirmation. Swanson leapt over the edge of the ship and right onto Jok as they approached. The two men wrestled on their feet like bulls locking horns. Swanson put his free arm around Zack and pulled him into a three-way crunch. Zack held his breath against the double rush of body odor.

So real Vikings belly bump, too. Great.

"This is Sven the Swede," Jok introduced him.

"I am Sven the Swede," said Sven. Zack nodded to him. "It is good you have arrived, Lost Boy. I can't carry these men much further on my own."

Jok roared with laughter and clipped Sven on the shoulder.

Like Swan from home, Sven favored his right leg but didn't seem to be slowed down by it. He began helping the tribe load their equipment onto the ship.

"Did you get it back?" he asked Jok quietly.

"Get what back?" Zack said.

Jok shook his head. "No, not today. But we had the Bears on the run."

45

Sven snarled at the mention of the Bears.

"We didn't find what we were looking for, and yet, found more than we were looking for," Jok said, pointing to Yggdrasil's Key in Zack's hand.

Sven looked at the key. "Ah well. Yggdrasil's Chest will be for another day."

"Yggdrasil's Chest?" Zack blurted out. "Is that what this key is supposed to open?"

"He doesn't know?" Sven said.

Jok shook his head somberly. "We should get back as soon as possible."

No one would answer any more questions as the tribes prepared to leave. Zack helped push both ships into shallow water. He climbed onboard Jok's ship, the one with the dragon head. He also noticed that Hilda and Helga had all the female fighters in their tribe. Maybe Jok was a little old-fashioned, just like Jock Gilman.

Everyone seemed to know exactly what to do. Several of Jok's men lifted up boards in the deck to reveal a huge storage area underneath. They pulled out dozens of oars, each one about twice Zack's height standing on end. Small wooden disks along the sides of the ship flipped up to reveal holes, each one just big enough for an oar handle. Shields, swords, axes, and spears were stowed and the deck replaced. Other belongings went into small chests that also served as rowing benches. Within minutes, the tribe sat in two long rows, one man per oar, ready to go.

Jok shook hands with the warrior sisters on shore. The

three of them were the last to board their longships before setting out. Zack stood in the back next to Sven, who kept his hand on a tiller to steer the ship as he called out.

"And . . . hoahhh . . . and . . . hoahhh."

The oars dipped and stroked in rhythm with his calls. The ship slowly backed up and then turned around. They were in a small bay. Zack could see just past its mouth where it opened up to a larger body of water. Hilda called out to her tribe as their ship navigated alongside.

Jok watched the water ahead. He stood at the front of the ship with his back to everyone. His cloak and his bushy red hair were all Zack could see. It was hard to imagine anyone but Jock Gilman standing there, not some look-alike Viking chieftain. Zack stared at him, trying to figure out how to even think about all of this.

It can't be anything but a dream. The coldest, smelliest, weirdest dream anyone has ever had. That must be it. So why doesn't that feel like the answer?

A crashing sound pierced his thoughts. Zack turned toward shore and saw a giant flaming ball hurtling through the air toward them. It landed in the water between the two ships with a huge, sizzling splash.

Zack pointed. "Look!"

A crowd of Bear soldiers was on the beach. They were loading a catapult device of some sort.

Jok was already at his side. "I see them," he said. "Infernal cowards. Keep her steady, Sven. Don't stop for anything."

"Should we raise the sail?"

"No. It could burn too easily."

Behind the Bears onshore, a smaller figure sat on horseback. He wore a deep red cape, the color of dried blood, unlike the Bears' dark fur cloaks. Beside him stood a short, squat creature. Zack recognized it right away. It was the one who had tried to take his key earlier. The creature waved a banner in the air, black on one side and red on the other.

One of the Bears put a torch to the catapult's payload. The catapult fired again. Another flaming ball shot out over the bay, straight toward Hilda and Helga. The missile just reached them and bounced off the side of their ship in a shower of sparks. Both twins fired back with a volley of arrows.

Sven continued to call out, faster than before. "And . . . hoahhh . . . and . . . hoahhh!"

The men strained against their oars. The ship picked up speed.

"What do we do?" Zack asked. If the ship caught fire, there wasn't going to be much choice but to jump into the freezing water.

Jok raised both arms and roared at the Bears. "Think again, weasels!"

"Should we go back?" Sven asked between calls. "Take them for all they're worth?"

"No," said Jok. "That's just what he wants. Another chance for that key."

Zack's hand tightened around the key.

Whoa. Hang on a second. This thing I'm never supposed to let go of? This is why we're playing flaming dodgeball?

"Don't worry," Jok said as if reading his thoughts. "You're safe."

Yeah. I feel really safe right now.

Zack kept his mouth shut, his fingers clenching and unclenching on the key.

The next missile was aimed at their ship. It landed close enough to douse several rowers with freezing cold water.

"What are they firing?" Zack asked. The charred ball seemed to be unfolding in a strange way.

"Bears," Jok said between gritted teeth.

"Bears?" Zack echoed, confused. But then he saw. It was bound with some sort of cord, but as it slipped beneath the surface of the water, Zack saw the shape of an arm, a hand. He took a deep breath and looked away.

"Incredible," Jok said. "Just like him to use his own fallen men. He knows nothing of right and wrong."

"Who?" Zack said. "The guy on the horse?"

Jok nodded. "Erik the Horrible."

Erik? Erik the Horrible? Let me guess. . . .

An unwelcome image of Eric Spangler's face stuck in Zack's mind.

It's official. This dream is now a nightmare.

The ship sliced through the water, faster than Zack ever would have imagined it could. They were soon out of the Bears' shooting range. Soon Erik and the others were just tiny figures on the beach.

Zack's heart slowly returned to normal speed. Jok quietly went back to his position at the prow.

When the two longships left the bay, they headed in opposite directions. Jok waved to the twins as they navigated to the left. Sven steered their ship up the valley to the right. As they moved through the small river, Zack saw narrow, winding waterways extending away from them in every direction like crooked spokes in a wheel. Squat, snow-covered mountains closed around them, and soon the other boat was out of sight.

As the men rowed, several of them kept looking over their shoulders at Zack. They whispered amongst themselves. Everyone seemed excited, but Zack only caught a few snatches of what they were saying.

". . . could be him."

". . . doesn't know about the prophecy."

"Yggdrasil's Key . . ."

Whenever Zack caught someone's eye, the man would turn back to his rowing without a word. Eventually, the only sounds were Sven's low calls and the light splashing of oars.

"Almost there," Sven said finally, just after sunset. "The *Winniferd* serves us well again."

Zack felt a sudden chill. "Winnifred?"

"Winni*ferd*," Sven corrected.

"Named after Jok's wife?" Zack asked, though he knew the answer. At least naming a boat made more sense than naming a Winnebago.

Sven nodded. "So you do know a thing or two, don't you,

Lost Boy? Yes, she disappeared from us—"

"Nine years ago," Zack said quietly.

Sven rubbed his beard. "That's right. Just like that. She set out hunting one morning and didn't come back. Jok searched for years. We all did. Finally, we had to move on. But Jok swears one day he'll find her. He's never given up hope." Sven clapped a hand on Zack's shoulder. "But I suppose you already knew that, too, didn't you, Lost Boy?"

Zack didn't answer. He stared straight ahead at the water, wondering if it was possible to be homesick in a dream.

The sky slowly turned from gray to black. Clouds blocked out any moonlight or stars. Zack could just see the land on either side of them. They seemed to be navigating up a narrow channel.

"Steady, steady, straight on," Sven called.

"How do you steer in here?" Zack asked.

He heard Sven breathe deeply through his nose. "Smell that goat dung? It takes us straight home."

Zack sniffed several times, but was glad not to pick up whatever scent Sven was following.

Soon, the glow of a fire on shore came out of the darkness. Zack could see buildings, but details were impossible to pick out.

As they drew closer, a small dock came into view. They coasted alongside it and came to a stop as the front end of the ship scraped softly against ground in the shallowest water.

The men set to work stowing the oars and unloading the ship.

"Welcome to Lykill," said Sven.

CHAPTER FOUR

Word of their arrival spread quickly. Soon, dozens of people were at the shore, carrying torches and clamoring to see Zack.

"Lost Boy!"

"Praise Thor, you have come!"

It quickly became embarrassing. Everyone was staring at him and he was starting to wish they wouldn't. It might have helped to know exactly what all the fuss was about. It was like he was a rock star but didn't know how to play any music. Zack looked at the ground as Jok shepherded him through the crowd and into the village.

They passed several crude wooden buildings, most of them with fences and small yards in front. People came out of their houses and the crowd grew. Zack smiled back at several of them. The attention was totally confusing, but it was hard not to get caught up in the excitement.

Soon they stopped in the center of the small village where a high bonfire was already blazing.

Jok turned to face the crowd. "Tonight," he shouted. With that single word, everyone grew quiet. Eager faces pressed in closer. Zack swallowed hard, not sure what to expect.

Jok held a fist over his heart and pulled down the corners of his mouth. "Tonight," he continued solemnly, "is a time for quiet reflection. I want you to go to your homes and think about what the arrival of Zack, the Lost Boy, means to you."

He held up Zack's arm by the wrist, with Yggdrasil's Key in the air. Zack heard a small gasp run through the crowd.

Jok went on. "I want you all to contemplate what this may bring."

Now everyone looked confused. They turned their heads and exchanged puzzled glances, murmuring quietly to one another. No one seemed to want to leave. Even Zack was a tiny bit disappointed. He had almost come to expect something more. This Jok was much more serious than his father.

Then Jok burst out laughing. He put a hand to his belly and roared like a crazed Santa. "I fooled you all! You should see yourselves. Did you think I had taken leave of my senses?" Several people nodded.

"Never!" Jok yelled. "Let the feast begin!"

Zack smiled broadly. Somehow, the familiarity of Jok's humor was a relief.

Soon the village was a hive of activity. The bonfire was stoked even higher, where Zack stayed warm while people came and went. Great troughs of meat and bread and cheeses were carried out of storage huts into various houses. Torches were planted in the ground, lighting up the small village square with a festive glow.

Many people stopped to shake Zack's hand and get a closer look at the key.

"So it's true," said one old woman, bending close to the key with wide eyes. Like everyone else, she was careful not to touch it. Zack smiled and offered awkward hellos, feeling like the world's most un-famous celebrity.

Several of Jok's men rolled a barrel over to where Zack stood. They pried it open and began filling long, pointed cups with a thick liquid of some sort.

Lars spoke loudly to Zack and everyone around them. "Lost Boy, when you tell your grandchildren about this day, I want you to say that it was Lars of Lykill who first raised his drinking horn to you in a proper welcome."

He held the horn up over his head. "To the Lost Boy!"

"To the Lost Boy!" echoed the others. Everyone with a drinking horn took a deep swig and then passed it to the person next to them. Eager for anything at all to eat, Zack gratefully accepted Lars' horn and took a gulp. A syrupy, thick liquid filled his mouth and burned his throat. He gagged, and sprayed the remaining mouthful out through his lips.

"What is that?" he choked.

Lars nodded, the white goop still dripping from his beard. "Good, huh? Goat's milk."

"Just goat's milk?" Zack was trying not to think about the little chunks in his mouth or the way his tongue was tingling.

"The best we have," Lars said. "Not a drop is poured until it has soured for at least seven days." He took the horn from Zack and raised it again.

"To the key!" he shouted. He downed the rest in a few huge swallows, stopping only at the end to spit out a mouthful as Zack had done.

A dozen others did the same and soon the air around the bonfire was filled with a pungent, rotten-smelling spray. Someone handed Zack another horn. He tried not to gag as he quietly poured it out on the ground behind him.

Please tell me there's something more to eat here than rotten goat's milk.

Before long, Jok retrieved Zack and led him through a low door into one of the wooden houses.

"Welcome to my home," said Jok.

The house was dimly lit and filled to capacity with people. The whole place was one long, windowless room about the length of a bowling alley lane.

One of the first things Zack noticed was the smell of smoke and cooking meat. A huge slab was sizzling on a spit over an open hearth in the center of the floor.

Food! Thank you, thank you, thank you, thank you.

The next thing he noticed was that his sister was the one doing the cooking. Zack was almost getting used to the familiar faces now, but it still made him laugh to see someone who even looked like his sister, cooking. Valerie Gilman was maybe the only person Zack knew who was a worse cook than their father.

Currently, her look-alike was the only person not staring at Zack; she was bent over the meat, poking it with a long fork.

"Valdis!" Jok called. "He is here!"

"Hello," Valdis said, still not looking up.

"Hi," said Zack.

"When can we expect to eat?" Jok asked. "I'm sure Zack is hungry."

"It will be soon," Valdis snapped back. "The food cooks no faster for the Lost Boy than for anyone else." She looked Zack briefly in the eye. Zack forced himself not to look away.

Jok ripped a loaf of bread in half and handed one piece to Zack. He pointed to Valdis and made a face that said "better not mess with her right now." Zack nodded in return. He knew just what Jok meant.

In the front of the house where they stood, shelves lined the walls top to bottom. The shelves were filled with dozens of sacks and buckets and all sizes of earthen jars.

The center of the house was dominated by the hearth. Smoke from the cooking fire escaped not through a chimney but through open triangular holes at either end of the peaked roof. Zack also saw a half-finished tapestry mounted on a tall loom that leaned against the wall. It was woven from the bottom up, showing the image of a man's feet and legs. The image stopped abruptly where the weaving was unfinished.

"Is that going to be you?" Zack asked.

Jok shook his head. "It is Thor, the mightiest of all gods. The one who watches us in battle. My wife will finish it when she returns. Now come, follow me."

Zack knew better than to ask any more questions. Apparently, the unfinished tapestry had sat there for nine years since Winniferd disappeared. At least Jock had accepted that his wife was gone. Zack felt a pang of sympathy for his father's Viking twin, who obviously still couldn't face that fact about his own wife. He followed Jok to the rear of the place, which was partitioned off by a wooden half-wall. A heavy bedframe covered with animal skins stood in the back corner. Two posts at the head of the bed were each topped with a carved dragon head, like small versions of the one on Jok's ship. This end of the house was also strewn with barrels and stacks of crates and tools. On the wall hung a round shield. It was painted with the same yellow-and-white diamond pattern as the banner Zack had seen them carry into battle just that afternoon.

The wall also held another large tapestry. Its pattern was a twisting mass of branches curving over and through each other in every direction. Zack noticed that it was the same kind of pattern as the one carved into his key.

He held the key up and examined it again. Jok nodded. He seemed to know what Zack was thinking.

"There are many things we should discuss."

"So . . . ?"

"First thing tomorrow."

"But—" Zack started.

"What?" said Jok. "Even the Lost Boy must enjoy a feast from time to time. Yes?"

"But I just—"

"Yes!" he shouted, lifting his arm in a wave to the whole room. Everyone raised their drinking horns, shouted back, and drank. No one seemed to know what they were drinking to, but it didn't seem to matter.

Jok turned back to Zack and pointed at the key and shook his finger. "Meanwhile—"

"I know, I know," Zack said. "Don't let it out of my sight." Apparently, Jok of Lykill was no easier to argue with than Jock Gilman of Minneapolis.

"Here," said Jok. He reached into a chest and handed Zack a piece of rough cord. "Good strong walrus skin, so there's no chance of losing it."

Zack threaded the rope through his belt loops and tied the big key securely at his side. As he moved back into the room, people started to laugh. Valdis looked at him and rolled her eyes. A little girl pointed at Zack and said, "Look mommy, just like you." Zack noticed that the girl's mother had a clutch of iron keys tied to her waist in the same way.

Soon everyone was laughing. Jok leaned over and whispered to Zack. "It is a sign of womanhood to wear keys in this way. It tells people that you are a farm mistress."

"Well, they know that I'm not," Zack whispered back. "Right?"

"Lost Boy, will you marry me?" someone cried out, and the crowd laughed even louder.

"It's all in fun," Jok said.

"Yeah, yeah," said Zack. "Give me a knife."

He shortened the cord and put the key back on around his neck. The cold metal hung heavily against his chest.

Well, at least I'll always know it's there.

When the food was ready, Jok made sure Zack got the first and largest portion of everything. He piled thick cuts of mutton and cheese onto a wooden plate and handed it to Zack, along with another half a loaf of bread. Zack found a seat and dug in.

People came and went, and so did all sorts of food. Apparently the feast was happening throughout the village. Most everything Zack saw was some kind of meat—whole chickens, giant roasts, slabs of fatty bacon. He ate with his hands, like everyone else. Sven sat next to him, his beard dripping with grease.

"You eat as much as Lars!" Sven grunted, through a huge mouthful of goat meat. Lars sat across from them with a full plate on his lap and a Fred Flintstone-sized piece of meat in each hand. He turned his head from side to side, chomping one and then the other. When he laughed, bits of meat flew out of his mouth like confetti.

"And you are almost as big as Jok!" Sven continued.

"Everyone says I'm going to be even bigger than him when I'm done growing."

"Who says?" Sven asked.

Zack realized he had been thinking about his own father. "Oh, uh, no one," he said, and took another bite. At least he wasn't freezing or starving anymore.

Valdis came over carrying a platter. "My father said to bring you more," she said, rolling her eyes. She picked up a piece of fish with her free hand and plopped it onto Zack's plate. Then she reached into a pouch at her side, and sprinkled a fine brown dust over the fish.

"What are you doing?" Zack asked.

"Spices," she said. "To improve the flavor." She looked him right in the eye.

"Spices?" Zack narrowed his eyes.

"Well, if you don't care to eat anymore—" she said, and reached for his plate.

"No, no, it's fine. Thanks." Zack took a big bite of the fish. He was hungrier than he was suspicious. And he hated to admit it, even to himself, but Valdis was a good cook. Clearly, not *everything* was the same here as it was at home.

Valdis smiled with her mouth but not her eyes, and moved on.

Music began filtering into Jok's longhouse from outside. At the sound of it, most of the crowd headed out the door. Zack took his plate and followed along with Sven.

Several musicians were playing next to the bonfire. People danced and clapped their hands. It was a sweet melody, unlike anything Zack had heard before, played by a light drum, a wooden flute of some sort, and a harp.

When Zack saw the beautiful girl who was strumming the harp and tapping her foot, he nearly spit out his food. Not possible. *Ashley Williams* was here, too? She was dressed like the other Viking women, in a full-length pleated robe and a white rectangle of cloth like a long apron. However, her hair was very short, which was unusual. Ashley Williams at home had long hair, and so did all the other girls Zack had seen in the village. But this was definitely her.

"The one playing the harp—what's her name?" he asked Sven. The music and the clapping made it easy not to be heard.

"Ah," said Sven, "the Lost Boy has good taste."

"No, I was just . . . um, curious," Zack said, still staring at her. Two dancers went whirling past. Their shadows from the fire threw light and dark across the crowd.

"Her name is Asleif," Sven said. "It is a great honor for a village as small as Lykill to have such a talented young *skald*."

"A what?"

"*Skald*. She writes poetry and songs about our times, our struggles against the Bears of the North, and her own struggles against the Bears."

"Her own struggles?" Zack asked.

"Asleif was part of a small tribe in the mountains. The Bears destroyed their village. Anyone who was of no use to them was killed, including her parents. She was spared only to become a personal *skald* for Erik the Horrible." Sven spit out the name as if it had a bad taste.

"How did she end up here?"

"We freed several of Erik's slaves on our last raid. She told us her story, how she has no people, and she asked to come with us."

"So now she lives here." Zack said.

Sven nodded. "An accomplished *skald* like her would be welcome in any number of larger villages. She owes us nothing but chooses to stay."

Sven motioned to Jok across the crowd. He pointed to Zack and then jerked his head toward Asleif. Jok's face lit up.

"What are you doing?" Zack said. "Stop."

Jok stepped into the firelight and held up his hand for the musicians to pause.

"If I may be so bold as to ask," Jok called out, "perhaps our young Asleif would offer a song to welcome

Zack, the Lost Boy, to Lykill?"

Asleif bowed her head to Jok and began to strum. Sven pushed Zack forward and the whole village let out a whoop. As she began to sing, Zack stepped back into the crowd, grateful that the attention was now on someone besides himself.

The honor of our tribe,
the village Lykill, and our names
in the glorious halls of Asgard
shall blaze as the torch
of a thousand years
beyond generations
and bounds of time.

Zack found he was caught up in the sweetness of her voice and the intricacy of her playing. For a few moments, he forgot where he was and just listened. When she had finished, he cheered with the rest of the crowd. Asleif smiled modestly and gave a quick shy glance in Zack's direction.

Sven nudged him in the ribs. "Now's your chance, boy. She's a fine young woman. Reminds me a little of someone I knew myself once. We were out on a sail, well south of here, docked in a strange little town."

"Okay, I'll do it." Zack interrupted. He knew that if Sven the Swede was anything like Swan Swanson back in Minneapolis, there was no knowing how long the story would go on. Besides, after everything Zack had been through that day, it seemed like speaking to Asleif should be easy.

She looked up at him again. Zack managed to smile.

So far, so good.

He took a step toward her and then stopped. His insides jumped, but not in the Ashley Williams kind of way. The usual butterflies in his stomach felt more like a bunch of baby hamsters squirming and trying to get out. He put a hand to his middle and grimaced. Asleif looked over again. Zack turned and dashed in the other direction.

The privy was set well away from Jok's longhouse. Zack cursed the distance as he sprinted across the yard. He held his breath and let himself into the dark little hut of a bathroom.

This is the part they don't show you in the movies.

After his first trip to the privy, Zack found himself turning around for a second trip even before he was halfway back to the feast. Valdis's sarcastic smile flashed in his mind.

Spices, huh?

When he finally made it back to the bonfire, the crowd had thinned out quite a bit and the music had stopped. Zack looked around for Asleif but she was gone.

"Ah, the Lost Boy lost an opportunity," Sven said, coming over to him. "Don't worry. One opportunity often gives way to another. Sven the Swede knows these things. Why I remember a certain maiden . . ."

Zack spotted Valdis carrying a cauldron into the yard. "Excuse me," he said to Sven, who continued telling his story to the night air as Zack walked away.

"What was that you put on my food?" Zack asked quietly. He wasn't anxious for anyone to know where he had been the last half hour.

"Just my own mixture," Valdis said. "Perhaps you ate more than your share." Several pigs were sniffing at the pot she carried. She sloshed a foul-smelling mixture of water and fish heads onto the ground, and onto Zack's pant legs. "Watch your feet."

One of the pigs started chewing on the laces of Zack's boot.

"It looks like you've made a friend," Valdis said, walking away.

"Yeah, keep laughing," Zack called after her. "You're lucky I'm in a good mood right now." It felt just like the kind of argument he would have with his sister, except for the part about the large pig licking his ankles.

Suddenly, something else caught his attention. A red light flashed in the corner of his eye. He turned toward it and saw not one, but two red dots glowing in the darkness beyond the yard. They blinked once, and then again.

All of Zack's tired muscles tensed at once. He stood perfectly still. He could hear a low, congested breathing.

"Hello?" he said tentatively. The dots blinked out and disappeared. He heard light footsteps crunching away in the snow, and then nothing.

Zack tried to chase off thoughts of being ripped into pieces by some kind of laser-eyed giant bug in the night. But since anything seemed possible in this place, it was hard to relax. He turned and hustled back toward Jok's longhouse.

CHAPTER FIVE

Zack opened his eyes. He couldn't remember falling asleep, but now sunlight was streaming through the smoke holes in the corners of the ceiling. Fur tickled his nose. He was lying under a pile of animal skins. Jok had insisted he take the only bed in the house.

He squeezed his eyes shut, trying to fight off the realization that he was still here.

No, no, no. Home. Comfortable. Shower. Breakfast.

Please?

He opened his eyes again and groaned. Everything was the same.

Maybe I'm in a coma. Maybe I'm lying in a hospital in Minneapolis somewhere. Everyone's looking at me and crying.

Maybe I'm never going to wake up.

The thought sent a shiver down his spine.

Two things were for sure. One: He had never fallen asleep in a dream and woken up still in it. And two: He was hungry.

The only thing to do was to get up and keep going.

Okay, here we go. Really, really, really weird dream. Day two.

The house was empty. A pot over the fire was bubbling with a thick white mush. Zack's stomach sent up a rumbling complaint—*feed me*. Since he couldn't find anything else around, he scooped up a bowl of the gruel. It turned out to be a sort of chewy, flavorless oatmeal. He gulped it down as quickly as possible, trying to imagine it was soggy Cheerios, and wishing it were pancakes and sausage.

After he ate, Zack stepped outside and got his first daylight view of the village. The wooden houses seemed to be lined up in rows leading down to the water. Zack could see the *Winniferd* beached from where he stood. Many of the houses had fenced yards with chickens and goats running loose. Jok's house and yard seemed to be the largest, with the privy and what looked like a small barn toward the back. Several houses had sloped, turf roofs, with sprouts of dead grass poking through a thin layer of snow.

People waved and called out to Zack as he wandered toward the waterfront. Everyone was hard at work on one task or another. Several women were dying cloth in a large vat over a fire. A very large man with a staff was trying to herd several goats through a small gate.

"Did you have your breakfast, Lost Boy?" asked one young woman. She handed him a small loaf over her fence. It was slightly sweet and not nearly as much like sandpaper as the bread from the feast.

Zack thanked her and asked if she knew where Jok was. She pointed the way he had been going, toward the water.

Several small children ran after him. "Lost Boy! Show us the key, Lost Boy!" Zack took it out and held it up for them to see. None of them wanted to come too close.

"The key is very strong," one little girl said in a quiet voice.

Zack crouched down next to her. "Yes it is."

"You are going to save us from the Bears, aren't you?" she asked. It was barely a question. She seemed to have no doubt.

Zack wanted to tell her no, he had no idea why he was here, this was all a big mistake and he just wanted to go home. He looked into her big gray eyes and opened his mouth to speak.

"Sure," he said. "That's right."

At the waterfront, Zack saw that the village was on an enclosed bay. Steep hills surrounded them on two sides and Lykill sat in a small valley where the ground flattened out in between. Behind Zack, on the far side of the village, stretched an expanse of forest, with more hills beyond.

He waved to Jok, who was working with several men at the water's edge. Some were shaving the bark from a fallen tree with axes. Harald and a few others were using hammers to pound heavy iron nails into the frame of a new boat. This one was shorter and deeper than the *Winniferd*. Zack noticed that their tools were some of the same weapons he had seen them using in a very different way the day before.

Jok came over as soon as he saw Zack.

"Good morning! You sleep well," Jok said. "And late. We're already halfway to a new cargo ship."

"Well it was kind of a big day yesterday," Zack said.

"With more to come."

"Good. When can we—"

"Right now," Jok said. They sat down on logs next to a small fire. Both began to speak at the same time and

Jok motioned for Zack to go ahead.

Zack rubbed his forehead, trying to figure out where to start. "Let me ask you this. Do I look familiar to you?" he said. "Do I remind you of anyone?"

Jok stared at him. "You are the Lost Boy. Zack is what you call yourself."

"Yeah," Zack said. "But does the name Zack mean anything to you? Zack Gilman? Or Jock Gilman? Or Minneapolis, maybe?"

Jok laughed. "You speak in riddles. I'm sure there are many things you know that we do not."

Zack took a deep breath. "Okay." He took out the key. "How about this?"

"Yggdrasil's Key," Jok said. "That is what we have to talk about."

"Is there a lock somewhere? Something I'm supposed to open, or do with this?"

"It opens Yggdrasil's Chest," Jok said.

Zack sighed with relief. At least it was an answer. "Yggdrasil's Chest? Okay. What's in the chest?"

"That's what we will find out," Jok said, rubbing his hands together. "Its treasure is supposed to bring the favor of Thor and all the gods on those who find it. Whatever the treasure may be, the reward is glory."

"Why don't you just break it open?"

Jok shook his head. "We have tried many times. This is not an ordinary chest. Hammers and axes are useless. The chest opens with your key, and nothing else."

"So you're doing all this and you don't even know what's in there?" Zack asked.

"The prophecy does not tell what Yggdrasil's Chest holds. It only says that you will find it."

"Prophecy," Zack said. "That keeps coming up, too. What is this prophecy?"

Jok stood up. "We had always thought you would know about the prophecy when you came." He led Zack back into the village to his longhouse. Under the bed where Zack had slept was a wooden box. Jok pulled it out and put it on a table next to a lantern, which he lit.

"Is that Yggdrasil's Chest?" Zack asked.

"No," Jok said. "Yggdrasil's Chest has been stolen from us again."

"Again?"

"Yes. By the Bears. By Erik the Horrible. We have recovered it and lost it more than once. Now that the prophecy has begun, getting the chest back is our only hope. That is what we were trying to do yesterday when you appeared to us."

Jok opened the box on the table. It held a stone tablet the shape of a small gravestone, flat along the bottom and curved at the top. Rows of evenly spaced, angular symbols were carved on its surface.

"What is it?" Zack asked.

"This," said Jok, "is the prophecy."

Zack looked closer and realized that he could read the strange symbols as if they were English.

"Let me try something," he said. He took off the key

and set it down. The symbols didn't change but their meaning seemed to slip away from him. Now he just saw lines going up and down, side to side, and diagonally. Then he picked up the key. It was like putting on special glasses. The words on the stone were once again perfectly clear. Zack read them out loud.

Yggdrasil's Chest, Yggdrasil's Key,
And Lost Boy will unite as three,
Beginning then the glory quest
That opens with Yggdrasil's Chest.

Glory found is glory earned
And what is Lost must be returned.
Size of a man, this Boy will be,
And with him comes Yggdrasil's Key.

With the key there comes a price:
Courage, Faith, and Sacrifice.
The way is far, the road will bend
The Boy will lead until the end.

Zack stared at the words for a long time. "What does it mean?" he asked finally.

"It means that Erik the Horrible is losing sleep," Jok said with a sly smile. "And it means that we have to get that chest back."

"Erik knows about this, too?"

"Everyone knows the prophecy," said Jok. "It has been told since before I was born."

"How do I know this is even real?" Zack asked. "How do I know I'm not just dreaming you?"

Jok burst out laughing again, with a blast of mutton breath in Zack's face. "Lost Boy, we have waited a long time for you. I am quite sure you are real."

"Listen," Zack began. "Even if I am who you're looking for, I don't want to be on some quest. I just want to get back home." He stepped away from the table. "I don't think I can help you."

"Have faith, Zack," Jok said. "I know you can help us." He slapped Zack across the back so hard that Zack almost spit up his morning mush.

Jok continued to show Zack around the village. The barn in the back of his yard turned out to be a forge. Tools hung from the ceiling and walls—heavy hammers, iron tongs, and chisels. An open barrel held a collection of what looked like several unfinished swords. In the center of the room was a black iron anvil next to a large oven. Sigurd was stoking the fire when they came in.

"Ah, Sigurd," Jok said. "What do we have for today?" Sigurd pointed to one of the unfinished swords.

"Sigurd is a man of few words," Jok whispered to Zack as he took up the sword. "But a fine metalworker."

Jok turned the piece over. The metal was still rough and dark compared to the finished swords Zack had seen before.

"What should it be called?" Jok asked.

"Called?" said Zack.

"Any object of worth should have a good name," Jok said. "We name our weapons. We name our ships. It says that these things mean something to us. That they are worth remembering."

"We had a goldfish once," Zack said. "We called it Kitty."

"I call my sword Lightning," Jok said, "and my axe is Thunder, a humble praise to the mighty Thor but an impressive companion to my sword." He looked back to the unfinished one in his hand. "We will see what this one wants to be."

Zack watched as Jok and Sigurd began their work. Jok held the sword in the glowing fire with his tongs while Sigurd used a bellows to pump air into the oven. When the metal was red hot, Jok transferred it to the anvil and Sigurd handed him a short hammer from the wall. Jok swung at the blade several times. The red metal jumped slightly on the anvil with each ear-splitting pound.

When the sword had gone back to the fire and was ready a second time, Jok put the hammer in Zack's hands.

"Have a go," he said. "Aim for the edge of the blade."

"I've never done this before," Zack said, taking a step back.

"And after today, you won't be able to say that. Now swing."

Zack looked at Sigurd, who seemed to have no emotion whatsoever. Sigurd looked blankly back at him, waiting.

Zack raised the hammer to his shoulder and pounded on the blade once. It made a dull clunking sound.

"Try again," Jok said. "As if it means something to you."

He swung again, harder this time. The hammer connected with a satisfying clang. A small shower of sparks jumped off the hot metal. It felt good, and he hammered it again several times. Each swing was like connecting with a punching bag. He pounded out more frustration than he even knew he was carrying. When he was done, he stood panting with his hands on his knees.

"We may have to call this one Zack's Honor," Jok said, inspecting the edge. Sigurd nodded.

"Again?" Zack said.

"Give it a moment." Jok put the sword back into the fire. Zack stepped up and pumped the bellows while Sigurd brought more wood.

When the blade was once again on the anvil, Zack fired away with another round of hammering. Sweat poured down his face. His arm began to ache. And he felt better than he had in a long time.

As they carried the sword back to the fire, Zack noticed a red dot, shining like a laser, peeking in at them through a knothole in the wall. It looked just like what he'd seen the night before in the dark. As he watched, suddenly the dot blinked.

"There it is again!" he shouted.

As Zack turned, his hand connected with hot metal.

"Look out!" Jok yelled, a second too late.

For a moment Zack didn't feel anything—he just heard a tiny sizzle. Then an intense pain shot through his hand, quickly radiating through his entire body. Jok thrust the sword at Sigurd and grabbed Zack by the shoulders. He pushed Zack out through the door of the forge and forced his hand down into the snow.

Again, Zack felt nothing for a moment, and then the pain returned. It spread from his palm and seemed to cover his whole body with a sharp aching feeling. It was as intense, and as real, as anything he had ever felt in his life. And with the pain came an even sharper realization.

This isn't a dream.

"Zack, stay still!"

I am really here.

"Sigurd, come help me!"

This is really happening.

All at once, he believed it. And just as quickly, he realized:

I might never get home again.

His mind swirled out of control. He was barely conscious of several other people around him now. His vision swam and everything sounded as if it was on the other side of a door.

"Where's Jok?"

"He went to get the healer."

Burn.

Pain.

Stuck.

The ground tilted. Everything went white; and then everything was gone.

When he opened his eyes, he was indoors. He could smell smoke. He sensed people moving around. His sister's face loomed over him.

"Valerie?"

"He is awake," she said matter-of-factly.

It came back to him quickly. He was in Jok's longhouse again. His entire arm was throbbing.

Valdis stood over him mixing something in a small stone bowl.

"Mix it well, but hurry," Jok said. Valdis turned away and kept stirring.

Jok put a hand on Zack's shoulder. "She is a fine healer."

"Why doesn't that make me feel any better?" Zack mumbled. He tried to sit up.

"Lie still," Valdis barked.

Zack put his head back again.

Before, he had felt as if he was in the most realistic dream possible. Now it felt like a reality that was incredibly dreamlike. He had no proof, but it didn't really matter anyway. What choice was there but to just keep going? In that way, nothing had changed.

Zack motioned for Jok to come closer. "I saw something today," he whispered.

"What kind of thing?"

"Something was watching us through the wall. That's why I burned my hand. I saw it last night, too."

Jok stroked his beard, nodding. He blew his nose out on the dirt floor. "Good."

"Good?" Zack said. "What if it was a spy or something?"

"Spies are everywhere. Not all spies are looking out. Some are looking in."

Before Zack could say anything more, Jok got up and went to hurry Valdis. It seemed as though every hour in this place raised more questions.

Valdis came over and sat down. She turned a reddish-brown paste out onto a strip of cloth. She doubled the cloth and then used it to bind Zack's hand. He winced when she touched him but the pain stopped almost immediately.

"That's amazing," he said, wiggling his fingers. "Thank you."

"Try to be more careful in the future," she said. "These herbs are rare."

"Don't worry, Zack, you'll still have a nice scar," Jok said, helping him sit up.

"What good is a wound without a good scar to show for it, huh?" said Harald, who stood nearby. Zack suddenly realized that most of Jok's men were gathered around. Harald lifted his sleeve to show Zack a jagged mark running from his wrist to his elbow. "I got this from one of the Bears. It was the last thing he ever did in his life."

"Yes but look at this," Jok said. He pulled up his tunic and showed the mark of a huge gash across his wide back. "Now that is a well-placed scar," he said.

"Speaking of well-placed scars," Sven said. "Hey, Sigurd, show us all your behind!"

Sigurd let out a huge burp in response and everyone burst out laughing.

Zack shook his head. In some ways, this place didn't feel so different from home.

"That's nothing!" Sven cried. He stood up on a bench

and let out a loud shot of gas at both ends at the same time. Valdis put both hands to her ears and left the house.

Soon everyone else was getting in on the action.

"Here you go, boys!" called Lars. He took a deep breath and belched out a string of syllables. "From. Land. To. Sea. We're. Bro. Thers. Allllllllll." The last belch was long and unmistakably musical.

"Lars the unbeatable!" Harald called out.

"What about you, Lost Boy?" Sven said.

Zack looked up. "What?"

"Care to join in?"

"No," Zack said. "No, I'm just—"

"Go ahead, Zack!" Jok shouted, reminding Zack more and more of his dad.

Zack was too weary to resist, just as he often was with Jock. Wait a second—that was it. Suddenly he knew exactly what to do. He held up his hand, and the men grew still. He took a deep breath and let it out in one long, enormous burp.

"V–I–K–I–N–G–S. Go. Vi. Kings. Let's. Go!"

The men went wild. "Zack the unbeatable!" Jok shouted. Several others started chanting. "Lost Boy, Lost Boy, Lost Boy!"

"Just something my father taught me," Zack said.

"What are these Vikings you speak of?" Sven asked when the chanting had stopped.

"What are Vikings?" Zack repeated. "Are you serious?"

"Yes, Lost Boy, tell us," said Harald.

"Well what do you guys call yourselves?" Zack asked.

"We call ourselves men of courage!" someone shouted.

"And faith!"

"And sacrifice!"

Everyone cheered their agreement and spontaneously started wrestling and crashing into furniture and one another. Jok put an arm around Zack's neck.

"That is what we call ourselves," Jok shouted over the noise. "As in the prophecy—we are men of courage and faith and sacrifice."

"Where I'm from, we call you Vikings," Zack said.

"Vikings," Jok said slowly. "It is a good word."

CHAPTER SIX

The next morning was different. Zack didn't expect to wake up at home. He opened his eyes knowing exactly where he was, though the familiarity was not much comfort. He sat up, thinking about bacon and eggs, electric heat, wool socks—and a change of clothes. He ran his tongue over his sandpapery teeth and even missed his toothbrush, sitting in a cup, next to a sink, in a bathroom, in some parallel universe hundreds of years away.

His father would no doubt be crazy looking for him by now. Zack shook his head, imagining police in the living room and news cameras on the front lawn.

He went off to get some bratwurst and just disappeared. Son, if you can hear me, just come home. I'll never make you go to another football game again.

He wondered if they were talking about him at school.

Yeah, I'm Zack's best friend, Ollie Grossberg. He always shares his lunch with me. He's the best.

He even let himself imagine that maybe, just maybe, Ashley Williams was thinking about him for the first time in her life.

Zack Gilman was always a mysterious, good-looking guy. Now I just hope he makes it back home again, so I can really get to know him.

Pieces of the puzzle floated through his mind—Yggdrasil's Chest, the key, the prophecy. The problem with this puzzle was that he didn't even know which pieces were supposed to fit—or how. Somehow, he had been brought here and somehow, he knew, he had to get home again.

After gulping down another bowl of barley mush, Zack went looking for Jok. He found him again at the boatyard. Several men were holding a long curved plank against the skeleton of the new ship, while others nailed it into place. A short mast had been crafted from a tree trunk. Harald was beginning an intricate design at its base with his carving knife.

"Good morning!" Jok roared over the pounding hammers.

"Listen," Zack shouted. "I was wondering—"

"Thundering, yes!" Jok yelled back. "Quite a noise!"

"No," said Zack, "I was *wondering*. Can we row back to where you found me?"

"Pounding?"

"No! Where you found me!"

Jok shook his head and Zack sat down to wait. He peeled the cloth bandage from his hand. A thin scar crossed his palm but his hand barely hurt anymore. It looked as if he had burned himself a year ago.

When the hammering finally stopped, Jok came over. "Now, what were you trying to say back there?"

"I was thinking we could row back to the place where you found me. It might help."

"Help?"

"Help me get home again. Back where I came from." As

80

soon as he said it out loud, Zack realized the last thing Jok wanted was for him to go home. He suddenly felt foolish for even asking.

"It's too dangerous," Jok said. "If we're to find the Bears, it should be where they don't expect us."

Zack looked at the *Winniferd* with its forty-eight oars. He thought about the maze of waterways that led away from Lykill. Sailing by himself was out of the question.

"Besides," Jok said, "You're needed elsewhere. We want you to—"

"Look out!" Harald shouted.

A fist-sized rock came whizzing through the air. Zack ducked just in time.

Thwack! Jok caught it like a fastball while staring intently up the shoreline. Zack followed Jok's gaze, wondering if another rock was coming. Fifty yards or so away from them was an inlet where a stream flowed into the bay. The inlet had a steep bank with what looked like a small cave dug into the side.

From inside the cave, two red dots stared out.

"That's it . . . or him . . . or it!" Zack said. "That's the thing I saw!"

Jok seemed not to hear him. He was already halfway to it.

"Wait! What are you doing? Are you crazy?"

Jok obviously didn't care. Zack ran after him, keeping several yards behind.

When he got to the stream, Jok shouted out. "Olaf! Come out of there!"

As Zack watched from a distance, the two red dots

blinked and disappeared. A meek voice came from the darkness. "Olaf not home now."

"Come out of there now, you slimy toad!" Jok growled.

A gray head emerged. Its pointed ears twitched side-to-side, seeming to test the air. The laser red eyes glanced up at Jok.

"Give it to me," Jok demanded.

The thing stepped out of its cave. It stood about three feet tall and wore no clothes. Its shiny gray skin looked damp and sticky. One hand was behind its back, concealing something.

"Yes, yes. Olaf here now," it said.

"Give it to me," Jok growled a second time.

It handed over what looked like a double-headed slingshot made from a tree branch with forks at both ends and a long leather strap.

"Was testing," Olaf said. "Rock should go there." He pointed upstream into the woods. "Still need some work." He smiled up at Jok. A thick rope of drool escaped between his gapped teeth.

"We need to keep you busy. An idle troll is a dangerous troll," Jok said, shaking his head.

Olaf stood up straighter. "Trolls always dangerous."

There was something familiar about Olaf. The small eyes, the ears that stuck out like open car doors, the strange sort of confidence. Even the drool. Zack's mouth dropped open when he suddenly realized.

Ollie.

Zack stared hard, his jaw hanging slack. The similarity was unmistakable now.

My best friend from home is a naked little troll.

"Go get ready," Jok told Olaf. "I have a mission for you."

Olaf disappeared back into his cave and Jok looked at Zack. "A mission for both of you."

Zack gulped. "Me?"

Jok nodded. "Now that you have come with the key, we are more powerful than ever. We are also more vulnerable. It is time we recovered Yggdrasil's Chest once and for all."

Olaf emerged wearing a tattered brown and green cape. *Camouflage*, Zack noted.

"The Free Man has returned?" Olaf asked.

"Precisely," Jok answered. "I saw his white falcon fly over this morning."

"Who's the Free Man?" Zack asked.

"He knows more about the prophecy than anyone. If you show him the key, he may be able to help us. Find out everything you can."

"Who else is going?" Zack asked.

"No one."

"What?"

"The Free Man is a hermit. He has no tribe and he comes and goes as he pleases. It is best to approach him quietly. I was going to send you with Harald, but you will be better off with Olaf. You'll have less chance of being seen or captured."

"Captured?" Zack tried not to sound as nervous as he was starting to feel.

"And Olaf is very good at not being seen," Jok continued.

Olaf picked some kind of bug out of his ear. He put the bug in his mouth and chewed slowly. Jok put a hand on Zack's shoulder and leaned in close. "You should have nothing to worry about."

Zack couldn't tell which was making his stomach feel worse—the idea of this mission, Olaf's bug chewing, or Jok's breath in his face.

"If anyone asks, you are young apprentices bound for Hedeby, nothing more," said Jok. "For this reason, I must ask you to travel without weapons. Swords raise too much suspicion."

"What about the key?" Zack asked. "The Bears know what I look like, they know about the key, they know everything."

"They also know that the key protects itself," Jok said.

Zack nodded, remembering the hairy creature that fought with the Bears, and the shock of electricity that had run through him when the creature tried to take the key.

Jok continued. "But that is no guarantee. We don't know enough about this key yet. Better to throw it in a bottomless pit and never see it again than allow Erik the Horrible to have it. You must be very, very careful not to be captured. Can we count on you?"

What, are you crazy? No, you can't count on me. I'm fourteen. I'm not even allowed to drive. How about YOU go out into the wilderness with no weapons and a three-foot-tall bodyguard?

Jok and Olaf were staring at him, waiting.

"What are our chances of finding this Free Man and getting back here without any trouble?" Zack asked.

Olaf had begun to step nervously from one foot to the other. "Should go soon, should go soon."

"Your chances are very good, if you stick to the mission," Jok said.

"Very good, but not great?" Zack knew he was looking for a guarantee that he wasn't going to get.

Jok looked at him. "I know you can do this."

Zack glanced down at the ground, feeling the back of his neck heat up. He'd never heard his own dad sound as confident in him being able to actually *use* his natural abilities as this man who barely knew him seemed to be. Zack took a deep breath, then another. "Okay, I'll do it." *Wait. Who said that?* "How soon until we have to leave?" *Shut up! Stop talking! Speak for yourself.*

"Excellent!" said Jok. "I knew we could count on you. You should go right away."

"All right," Zack said. *Hang on a second. I am speaking for myself. Shoot.*

Zack's heart fired like a machine gun. But the confidence Jok seemed to have in him was contagious. As he followed Jok and Olaf back toward the village, Zack couldn't help still thinking of his father.

Well, Dad, you always said I needed a little fire in the belly. I'm thinking this counts.

The feeling of readiness inside him was unfamiliar. Not what he would have expected. He was still terrified. His stomach still churned like a washing machine.

But Zack had also begun to realize he'd never get home by staying still. Maybe this was the way out.

❧

They set off to the north. Olaf led Zack away from the village and deep into the forest. A light snow blew around them, helping to erase any footprints they might have left in the shallow ground cover.

"Are you sure you know where you're going?" Zack asked. So far, he had only seen Olaf eat bugs, drool, and kiss up to Jok. "I don't think we're heading north anymore."

"Zack want to lead?" the troll said, with the same kind of calm coolness that Ollie showed once in a while at home. "Zack know about Bear traps? Zack look out for head cutters? Flying spears? Hidden pits?"

Clearly, Olaf was smarter than he looked, just like Ollie. "I guess not," Zack said. "Keep going."

The troll's short legs made it easy for Zack to keep up. Every hundred feet or so, Olaf would hawk a glob of yellow spit onto the ground or the side of a tree, sniff it, and move on. Sometimes Zack got out of the way in time. Sometimes he didn't.

"What are you doing?" Zack asked, wiping off his shoe for the third time.

"Scent mark," said the troll. "For most, is invisible. For Olaf, will lead back to Lykill."

"I don't know," Zack said. "Look what happened to Hansel and Gretel."

"Who?" Olaf said.

"Forget it." He changed the subject. "Hey, Ollie—I mean, Olaf. You said this Free Man knows all about the key, right?"

Olaf spoke without stopping or turning around. "Many things, yes,"

"Do you think he might know how I could use it to get home again? Jok didn't seem too interested in that subject."

"Home?" Olaf asked.

"Yeah, back to Minneapolis, where I'm from." Zack picked up a dead branch for a walking stick. "Where my father and sister live."

After a long pause, Olaf spoke again. "Olaf thought Lost Boy was orphan, like Jok."

"Jok's an orphan?"

Olaf nodded. "Tiny Jok baby, left in Lykill by no one knows who. Raised here but not from here."

It struck Zack as odd. His father wasn't an orphan, and even though Zack knew that Jock and Jok weren't the same person, he realized how much he had started to lump them together in his mind.

He shook it off. "So anyway, do you think the Free Man might help?"

"Could be," Olaf said. "Free Man knows much things."

After several hours of hiking, they came to a break in the woods. Olaf stopped short and put up his hand for Zack to wait, then motioned for him to come closer. Zack ducked down behind a large fallen pine tree. The troll stood on tip-toe to see over the top of it.

A cluster of tents was set up in the middle of a field. Large bonfires burned at either end of the camp. Next to one of them were several deer carcasses strung up on high poles. Bear soldiers were everywhere. Sword-carrying sentries circled the perimeter.

Zack and Olaf spoke in low whispers.

"Why didn't anyone tell us this was here?" Zack asked.

"Is new camp," Olaf answered. "Is much very closer than before."

"There must be at least a hundred soldiers here," Zack said. "What do we do now?"

Olaf put his hands to the sides of his head. He closed his eyes halfway and began mumbling. *"Mashen, kuntara, mikmik, kuntara, fa."*

"Olaf?"

The troll didn't answer. He seemed to be in some sort of trance. After a minute he opened his eyes. "Is memory chanting," he explained. "Is ancient Troll technique for remember. For telling all later."

"Cool," said Zack. "I could use that for school."

Several soldiers dragged a man into the center of camp, stopping in front of a large tent with the Bears' black and red banner flying from its peak. The man was bound at the wrists. His slumped head was covered with black marks. It looked as if his hair had been burned off.

The man put up no resistance. They forced him to kneel on the ground and removed the last tatters of his bearskin cloak. Zack could see the lash marks on his skin.

The tent flaps parted and out stepped Eric Spangler's

double. Olaf breathed in sharply.

Zack didn't need to be told who it was. "Erik the Horrible," he whispered.

His hair was longer than Spangler's, but even from nearly fifty yards Zack recognized the familiar sneer and the overconfident swagger. Erik's red cloak was trimmed in fur and what could only have been bones clattering along behind him. He carried a brightly burning torch on the end of a carved metal staff.

The hairy sidekick who'd attacked Zack in his first battle was there, too. One of his arms hung normally to the side, but now Zack could see that the other arm faced in the opposite direction, as if he had been taken apart and put back together incorrectly. He ambled along beside Erik, nodding a lot and swinging a large axe with his backward arm.

"Got it," Zack muttered to himself. "Doug Horner with fur."

"Is Orn," Olaf whispered. "Is right-hand Ogre to Erik the Horrible. Is not too bright."

Erik was yelling orders and pointing a lot. He tipped his torch and held it under the soldier's chin. The man reeled back with a cry.

"What are they going to do?" Zack asked, afraid that he already knew. He started to stand up but Olaf pulled him back down.

"Move less. Could be Zack there instead."

Erik barked another order and Orn stepped in. The kneeling soldier shuddered as Orn raised his axe, backward over his head. Zack squinted, not wanting to watch but unable to look away. Orn brought the blade down with a heavy swing, missing the soldier completely and catching himself square-ly on the foot. With a piercing howl, he leapt back. A thick green liquid oozed from his wounded foot. Several hairy toes lay scattered on the ground.

"Oh man," Zack whispered, holding his stomach. Still, he couldn't stop watching.

Erik reached out and rapped Orn on the head with the butt of his metal staff. He pointed to the soldier. Orn hopped on one foot, trying to pick up his axe again.

"What about those toes?" Zack asked.

"Is all the time for Orn," Olaf whispered. "Is helped by Ogmunder the Wizard. Ogmunder make new Orn parts. See arm? Sometime not so good."

"Ogmunder?" Zack said.

Olaf nodded.

Ogmunder. The name was too similar for doubt. His prin-cipal, Mr. Ogmund, the only person who could possibly make things worse than they already were, was some kind of wizard, lurking around this world somewhere. Great.

Zack strained forward to get a closer look. He turned his ear toward the camp to try and hear what Erik was saying. He could almost make out their words.

Without warning, his foot slipped and he lurched for-ward. He fell over the log for a moment and scrambled back out of sight. But it was too late.

CHAPTER SEVEN

A shout came up from one of the sentries. Several Bears pointed toward the woods.

"Go time," Olaf whispered.

Zack stayed low as he followed Olaf silently back into the forest. They hadn't gone far when a splintering sound broke the air. The underbrush crackled, the ground opened up, and Olaf disappeared into a pit.

Zack dove to catch him a second too late. "Olaf!" he whispered fiercely. He had seen this kind of thing on bad TV shows, and it had always seemed so fake. Now Olaf was ten feet below and out of reach.

Olaf spoke in low tones. "Is any soldiers?"

Zack looked back. Two Bears were crossing the field toward the woods. "Two of them, coming this way," he said, his heart pounding. It was hard to keep quiet.

"Go," said Olaf. "Go now."

"No," Zack said. "Throw me your cape!"

"Go!" the troll hissed. Zack only reached out his hand in reply.

Olaf slung his cape up the wall of the pit. Zack caught it and wrapped the end tightly around his hand. "Now grab on and climb."

Olaf jumped up and grasped the edge of the cape. There was a tearing sound and he fell back down with a handful of cloth. Zack stretched his arm as far into the pit as it would go. "Again!" he shouted. "It has to be now!" There was no need for whispering anymore. He could hear the soldiers, almost to the edge of the forest.

Olaf jumped up and grabbed on. The cape held. He braced his legs against the earthen wall of the pit and pulled himself up. Zack crawled backwards, pulling as hard as he could.

"Come on, come on, come on!" he said. He stood up and gave one last big pull. Olaf came flying out and Zack went flying backward. For a moment they were a tangle of cloth and bodies. Just as they scrambled to their feet, the two Bears burst into the woods.

"Go!" Olaf shouted.

Zack took off. He hadn't gotten far when he remembered the troll's short legs. He turned around. Olaf was now about halfway between himself and the approaching Bears. With a rush of adrenaline, he ran back. As the first Bear approached Olaf, Zack approached the Bear. The Bear raised his sword high. At the last second, Zack bent forward and pummeled the Bear in the stomach, using his head like a human battering ram. Somehow Zack kept his feet. The Bear went shooting back, knocking himself and the other soldier to the ground.

Zack didn't stop to watch. He grabbed Olaf under both arms, lifted him up, and ran.

"This way go!" Olaf shouted. "Now right go! Yes! And left go!"

Zack held him against his own chest with one arm, and ran with the other fist pumping. Branches whipped him in the face. A trickle of blood ran into his eye. He listened to Olaf and sprinted blindly, following the troll's directions.

The soldiers growled as they followed: "Don't lose them," one said. Their voices and footfalls grew closer and closer.

"Where are we going?" Zack gasped.

"To the Free Man go!" Olaf shouted. "Run!"

Zack didn't even have time to think. Suddenly the forest opened up and there was no ground beneath his feet. A frozen lake spread out below them. Zack let go of the troll, pinwheeling his arms to keep from flipping over in the air as he fell. Their bodies broke through the ice with a muffled splash and Zack was instantly submerged in freezing cold water. He had no time to catch his breath. He had no sense of up or down. His lungs screamed for air as he struggled to find the surface.

Suddenly, his head hit an icy ceiling with a painful thud. He pushed against it with his hands. It didn't budge. He pounded with his fist. A low cracking sound vibrated through the water, but the ice held. He felt his strength draining away and his vision began to fade.

Just as everything was starting to go black, something tugged at his collar. Zack felt himself pulled along the under-side of the ice. He reached up and felt Olaf's small hand pulling him with surprising strength. Finally, he burst out of the water, spitting and gasping for air.

"Thanks," he sputtered between coughs. It was all he

could manage to say, but it registered with Zack that Olaf had just saved his life. Another minute and it could have been the Bears pulling him from the freezing water, alive as their captive—or dead.

There was no time to rest. The Bears were still coming. Zack and Olaf scrambled to their feet.

"Don't stop, no!" Olaf urged. They slid along the ice to the shoreline. It was a shallow beach, no more than a few feet, rimmed by a high rocky wall. Where Zack and Olaf had taken the fast route through the air, the two Bears were climbing carefully but steadily down the wall toward them.

"I'm starting to really hate these guys," Zack said between chattering teeth.

"We run more now!" Olaf shouted.

They had barely turned to go when they saw the wolves, six or eight of them moving slowly up the beach. They seemed to be looking Zack in the eyes.

"I don't know a lot about wolves," said Zack. "But I'd say these guys look hungry."

One of the Bear soldiers jumped the last ten feet to the ground, followed by the other. They stood with hands on swords, keeping back and eyeing the pack of wolves.

Zack knew without trying that the lake ice was too thin for them to escape in that direction. The Bear soldiers blocked their way up and out; and the wolves were closing in from the other side.

"Any ideas?" he asked Olaf.

Before Olaf could answer, the wolves began to growl and

bark. As a pack, they paused, lowered their heads, and then sprinted right toward Zack and Olaf. Zack had no time to react. He braced himself, waiting for the first shock of sharp teeth. But the wolves ran right past them and moved in on the Bears. The Bears leapt back to the wall and started madly climbing. The pack reared onto their hind legs, leaping and gnashing their teeth, scarcely missing the soldiers. Zack watched as the Bears reached the top of the cliff and fled back into the woods.

Another growl sounded from behind him again. Zack whirled around, expecting more wolves. Instead, he saw a person standing on the beach.

"The Free Man!" Olaf cried.

The stranger held up his hand in greeting. He let out another, softer growl, and the wolves ran to him like obedient dogs. They sat in a cluster at his side. Olaf and Zack followed cautiously behind.

The Free Man was young; not much older than Zack. He wore a simple woolen cloak and heavy trousers bound with criss-crossing leather straps to the knee. Zack had imagined that this wise hermit would be an old bearded man with a tall wizard's hat, or something like it.

"Hello, Olaf," said the Free Man, and then, "Welcome, Zack."

Welcome, Zack?

"How do you know my name?" he asked.

"Knows many things, the Free Man," Olaf said, shaking the Free Man's hand vigorously.

"We must go," the Free Man said. "They will be back with others. Come. It is warm in my cabin."

At the word "warm," Zack suddenly realized how miserably cold he was. His wet clothes were starting to freeze and stiffen up. The Free Man wrapped the two wet travelers in his cloak and set off. They followed him and the wolves through a narrow pass in the rocks and up a steep trail. It was clumsy going, with Zack towering over Olaf inside the cloak and trying not to trip over him as they went along the rocky path.

"Careful," the troll admonished. "Is too big sometimes Zack," he muttered to himself.

"I heard that," Zack said. "Maybe Olaf is too small."

The Free Man stopped and turned to them. He wore the expression of a kindergarten teacher trying to make something very clear. "Travel quietly," he said. "You do realize we may be followed and that this is a dangerous place?"

"It wasn't me," Zack objected.

The Free Man cut him off with a sharp glare.

"Sorry."

Zack scowled down at the lump of cloth that was Olaf at his side. They traveled the rest of the way mostly in silence. All Zack could think about was food and fire as they hiked upwards.

Pancake sandwich. Cheese enchilada. Meatloaf.

He felt a poke in his side and then heard Olaf, speaking low. "Zack's stomach growling in Olaf's ear."

"I can't help it," he whispered back.

The Free Man's cabin stood in a clearing on the edge of a high cliff. Zack's heart dropped when he saw it. The entire building, from rooftop to front door, was made of ice. Like the houses in Jok's village, it had no windows. The walls were a cloudy white, offering no view of the inside.

"How warm can it be?" Zack wondered aloud.

"Come in," the Free Man said. He spoke quietly to the wolves and bowed his head in their direction. One of them responded with a soft huffing sound, then turned and led the pack back into the woods.

Zack ducked through the front door and was shocked to see a fire blazing in the ice-carved hearth. He and Olaf stood next to it, hungrily soaking up the warmth. His clothes began to melt and drip. Everything else stayed frozen solid.

An ice table and benches stood at the far end of the single room. Ice slabs served as shelves on the crystalline walls, which were finely etched from top to bottom with intricate designs. Amidst curving twisted branches like the ones on Zack's key, the carvings also showed dozens of wild animals, some of them unfamiliar, and each one somehow attached to the one next to it. From a snake's tail, the leg of a wolf formed. From the mouth of the wolf flowed a great winged creature with horns on its pointed head.

The far wall also had several lines of familiar symbols carved into it. Zack recognized them right away—the prophecy. The strange markings were as easy to read here as they had been on the stone tablet Jok had shown him in Lykill.

> *Yggdrasil's Chest, Yggdrasil's Key,*
> *And Lost Boy will unite as three . . .*

"How did you do all this?" Zack asked.

The Free Man was busily putting more wood on the fire. "We each have our own abilities," he said.

"Yeah," Zack said, "but still—why doesn't this all melt?"

"Because I don't expect it to."

"That's it?" Zack said. "You just expect it to stay frozen and it's that easy?"

The Free Man stopped stoking the hearth and looked at Zack. "I didn't say it was easy. Come, have something to eat."

He gave Zack and Olaf bowls of gray watery stew from a pot over the fire. It made Zack think of old soap, but he gobbled it down anyway. Olaf poured half of his bowl into Zack's and ate the rest slowly.

The Free Man offered Zack dry clothes but everything was too small. Zack wrapped himself in two scratchy blankets. His wet things and Olaf's cloak were hung next to the fire.

"They should be dry by tomorrow when we set off," the Free Man said.

"We?" Zack asked. "Are you coming back to camp with us?"

"Not go back to camp yet," Olaf said.

"What?" Zack said. "I thought we were supposed to talk to the Free Man and then report back."

"I'm not the one you want to speak to," the Free Man said.

Zack stopped, his spoon halfway to his mouth. "So we came here for nothing?" He could hear the tension in his own voice. "You haven't even looked at the key."

Olaf poked him in the side with a long finger. "Zack wait and Zack listen."

"It's not important that I look at the key, Zack," the Free Man said. "But I can still help you. Tomorrow we will seek out Huginn and Muninn."

Olaf breathed in sharply and clapped his hands. "Ah, Huginn and Muninn!"

"Only Zack," the Free Man said. "I'm sorry, Olaf."

Olaf immediately stopped clapping and slumped back down.

"Huginn and Muninn?" Zack said. "Who are they?"

The Free Man pointed to two birds with outstretched wings, etched into the wall.

"Birds?" Zack said incredulously. He walked over and examined the carving more closely.

"Ravens," Olaf said. "Is many things they know, like Free Man."

"They fly further than any animal or mortal being," the Free Man said. "They bring the news of the world back to Asgard every day."

Zack held up his hand. "Sorry, catch me up here. Asgard?"

"Asgard is the home of the gods. We live here in Midgard, which is the land of humans."

Olaf cleared his throat.

6/03

The Free Man nodded to Olaf. "Excuse me. Humans and others. This world, Midgard, is one of many worlds. Asgard is another."

"They sound like football positions," said Zack. "Midgard, Asgard, Left Guard, Right Guard, Tight End, Tackle, Quarterback . . ." He trailed off. Their blank faces told him he was the only one in on the joke.

The Free Man continued as if Zack hadn't spoken. "There is Jotunheim, where the giants live, and Niflheim, which is the land of the dead. Dwarves, elves, and others have their worlds as well."

YO-tun-haim. NIFF-el-haim. Zack repeated the strange names in his head, trying to commit everything to memory. "I didn't think things could get any weirder around here than they already were. I guess I was wrong; but why are you telling me this, anyway?"

"All worlds are connected to Yggdrasil," the Free Man said.

Zack's hand went to the key around his neck. "Yggdrasil's Key."

The Free Man nodded. "The key opens Yggdrasil's Chest, which was made from the wood of Yggdrasil."

Zack looked at the key again, at the pattern of branches and leaves. "Is Yggdrasil . . . a tree?"

Again, the Free Man nodded. "Yggdrasil is the heart of the universe. It grows through all worlds."

"It must be a big tree."

"Bigger than you can imagine. It grows everywhere. Its

three roots reach all the way to three different worlds—to Asgard, and to Jotunheim, and to Niflheim."

"Where are we going?" Zack asked.

"We are going to look for Huginn and Muninn in the branches of Yggdrasil itself. If there is anywhere in Midgard we will find them, it will be there."

As they spoke, the Free Man took Zack's bowl, refilled it, and set it outside the door. Zack saw a white falcon come in for a landing at the Free Man's feet.

"Do Huginn and Muninn know about the key?"

"More than most," the Free Man said, shutting the door. "If you can prove yourself, they may be very useful to you."

Zack groaned. "I knew there was a catch. What do I have to do to prove myself?"

"You have to find them."

"Huginn and Muninn?"

"Yes."

Zack spoke extra slowly, struggling to stay patient. "And how do I do that?"

"That is where I can help. We will leave first thing in the morning. It is a difficult trip."

"Oh, well," Zack blurted out, his temper suddenly rising, "it's been so easy this far. May as well get a little challenging, right?" He began to pace inside the cabin.

"I know you didn't choose this, Zack," the Free Man said quietly.

"That's right I didn't choose it," Zack snapped. "I have no idea how I got here or what I'm supposed to be doing, or how I'm ever going to get out of here again. Everyone keeps talking about 'the prophecy' this and 'the prophecy' that. I'm not some prophecy. I'm just . . . me. I don't know what everyone wants from me."

The Free Man put a hand on his shoulder. "And I'm going to tell you just what you don't want to hear."

Zack glared at him, but the Free Man just met his gaze calmly, and finally the anger drained from Zack's face. "What?" he asked.

"There is much more to do and you have to be strong," the Free Man replied. "Do you understand?"

Zack clenched his teeth and looked at the ground. "What if I'm not strong? What if I just say I'm done? Game over."

"No!" Olaf cried.

"You are free to make your own decisions," the Free Man said. "For now, it's late. Tomorrow you can decide what you want to do."

CHAPTER EIGHT

As Zack lay next to the fire in the Free Man's cabin, he tried to block out the question of what he'd do the next day, and just get some rest. He looked over at Olaf, curled up in a ball nearby and snoring.

I wonder what Ollie's doing right now?

Every time he closed his eyes, all he saw was images of home. Comfortable bed. TV. Full refrigerator. Jock, working on the Winnie.

Jock working on the Winnie?

It was a surprise to mentally land on his father like that. Zack had fantasized a million times about the day he'd leave for college, strike out on his own, get free of Minneapolis. Get free of Jock. He loved his dad, but they just didn't seem to fit together. Zack had always been convinced that a little distance between them would be a good thing. But suddenly the thought of his dad working on the Winnie was somehow comforting and painful at the same time. He actually *missed* being there—he missed his dad.

After a fitful night, he awoke at dawn. Olaf was still snoring, a small pool of frozen drool on the icy floor next to him. Zack dressed quickly in the cold air and went outside. The Free Man stood at the edge of the cliff, looking over miles of undisturbed forest and waterways. The low mountains in the distance were a pale lavender color in the light of the rising sun.

Zack cleared his throat. "Can those ravens tell me how to get home once all this is done?"

"I don't know," the Free Man said without turning around.

Zack looked out at the wilderness. A flock of birds flew silently past. He spoke again, quietly. "After we do this, can we have something to eat besides that hot dishwater you gave us yesterday?"

The Free Man turned and looked at him. For the first time since they had met, he smiled.

They left Olaf sleeping by the fire and walked uphill from the cabin. At the edge of the woods, the Free Man chittered at a squirrel on the side of a tree. The squirrel spoke back and the Free Man nodded his head.

He turned back to Zack. "That's good. No human has been this way all night."

"That's amazing," Zack said. "How many languages do you speak?" They left the clearing and entered a dense forest of pine and other, leafless trees. Bright sunshine turned to patterns of shade and light on the ground.

"I speak to all animals," the Free Man answered. "But it is not about language. It is about seeing them for who they are."

"Okay, Mister Mystical, here's another question for you. Do you ever answer anything directly?"

The Free Man stopped, turned to Zack, and looked him very seriously in the eye. "Yes."

Zack caught another tiny smile before the Free Man continued on.

"Well you've got a sense of humor, that's good. But seriously, where are you from? How do you know all this stuff?"

"My story is my own, and believe me, not nearly as interesting as yours. I keep to myself and I help where I can."

"Help anyone? Everyone?" Zack pressed.

"I help those who believe in freedom. Under Erik the Horrible, no one would be free. He would enslave humans and animals alike."

Zack thought about all the animals in Jok's village. "I probably shouldn't say this, but what about Jok's goats and chickens and everything? They're kind of enslaved, too."

"That's true," the Free Man said. "Jok's tribe kills other animals for their flesh and their skins, as do other people of this world. I wish this were not the case. But sometimes one must choose the greater good over having everything as it should be. What Jok does for his people, Erik the Horrible does for power, and for pleasure."

They pushed upward through snowy forest. Zack had imagined that the Free Man's cabin was at the top of a mountain but they climbed steadily higher. The effort helped Zack stay warm but he noticed that he wasn't nearly as out of breath as he might have been even a week ago. He kept pace with the Free Man, shoulder to shoulder.

Soon they came to a cave in the side of the mountain.

The opening was almost a perfect circle, as if it had been cut into the rock by hand. The darkness beyond showed no clue as to the size of the cave. Draped over the mouth was a huge gray and tan snake, at least as long as Zack was tall. Zack stopped short when he saw it.

The Free Man hissed a quick exchange with the snake. Then he turned to Zack. "This is our way, but first you must show her the key."

"I thought snakes didn't come out in the winter," Zack said.

"Is that important right now?" the Free Man asked.

Zack shrugged. "Good point." He reached into his shirt and held the key up. The snake let out a long hiss and cocked its head to the side as if it were considering something. Then it spoke.

"So it's true. The Lost Boy has arrived."

"Hey, I can understand you!" Zack said. He turned to the Free Man. "I can understand it . . . him . . . her?"

"You'll find this part of the woods a bit different than the rest of Midgard," the Free Man said. "Go ahead. Say hello to her."

The snake was watching Zack. She seemed to be expecting a response.

Zack spoke carefully. "Uh, hello. My, name, is, Zack."

"No need to go so slow. I'm a snake, I'm not hard of hearing," she answered.

Zack blushed. "Oh, sorry. Well, um . . . could we please go through?"

"I'll need the key first," the snake said.

Zack looked at the Free Man. The Free Man looked back at him blankly, offering no suggestion.

"I can't," Zack said.

"Give it to me," she said, more sharply than before.

"No," Zack said right away. "I can't."

The snake slid down the side of the cave and curled itself around Zack's ankles, hugging tightly. "Good. As it should be."

Zack fought the impulse to jump back, not because he was afraid but because somehow it seemed rude to do so.

The snake looked up at him. "Before you may pass, I have two questions for you. First you must tell me: What will my first question be? And second: What will be the answer to my first question?"

Zack stood very still and thought. It was impossible to do anything but stand still with the snake around his ankles. The Free Man stood to the side, saying nothing.

A light bulb of inspiration went off in Zack's head. "I think I know."

"Yes?" the snake said.

"The answer to the first question is 'What will my first question be?,' because that's the first thing you asked me. And the answer to the second question is 'What will my first question be?,' because that's the answer to the first question."

The snake loosened her grip. "You are clever, Lost Boy. You can think on your feet. That may serve you well." She slithered back to her spot over the mouth of the cave.

"Thanks," Zack said, and then, because he couldn't resist asking, "Aren't snakes supposed to go *sssss* a lot?"

The snake rolled her tiny eyes. "Travel sssssssafely, Lossssst Boy," she said sarcastically. "There. Happy?"

Zack blushed a second time. He and the Free Man thanked the snake again and stepped inside the cave. It turned to the left almost immediately. Soon they were in pitch blackness. Zack felt his way along the rough stone walls.

"Am I going to fit through here? How small does it get?"

"I don't know," the Free Man said from several feet ahead. "Step carefully."

They made their way in silence for several minutes. A soft breeze blew through the cave, carrying a musty smell, like rotting leaves. Suddenly, the passage opened and there was no wall on Zack's right. He was glad for the extra room but his relief only lasted for about three seconds. He heard some pebbles loosen under his foot and fall off the path, followed by a long, long silence, and then a faint splash far below. He pressed his left hand harder against the passage wall trying to find something to hold onto.

"Where are you?" Zack called.

"Still here," the Free Man said. His voice was small, alarmingly far ahead.

"Wait up!"

"Take your time. Move slowly. I can see a light up ahead."

If the Free Man had been able to get that far, then Zack could, too. He took a deep breath. The tiny shift in his body weight as he exhaled caused his right foot to slip sideways.

"HEY!" His body stumbled through darkness. He came down hard on the rough floor. His chin scraped across the rock as his own momentum carried him over the edge.

"Free Man! Help!" His feet dangled in nothingness and kicked at air. The ledge where he had been standing was apparently like a shelf, with only space underneath. Zack pressed his hands into the sharp rocks and managed to find a handhold. If he pressed hard with his arms, he thought, he might be able to pull himself back up. Then he heard a squeak. Something scrambled over his arm. He felt the sharp sting of tiny teeth on his thumb.

"HEY!" he yelled at the rat, or whatever it was. For the smallest instant, it made him angry to be nibbled at such an inconvenient moment. Then he remembered to be terrified again.

"FREE! MAN! NOW!" he screamed, using all the lung power he could muster.

"I'm here," the Free Man said from right above him.

Zack heard another squeak and felt another little chomp on his finger. The Free Man squeaked back urgently, and the biting stopped. The Free Man grabbed Zack under each arm and pulled hard. Zack moved about an inch further onto the ledge.

"You are heavier than you look," the Free Man grunted.

"Is that important right now?" Zack said between gritted teeth.

A few more pulls and Zack rolled onto the ledge. He lay

on his side, pressed against the wall, catching his breath.

"You scared him," the Free Man said.

"Who?"

"The rat."

"I scared him, huh? Well, tell him I'll try to yell more quietly next time I'm falling off a cliff."

The Free Man squeaked a few more times, and Zack heard what sounded like a tiny "hmph!" before the rat scurried away again.

A few minutes later they emerged into the light of the forest. Zack took deep, hungry breaths of the fresh air.

"Keep going," the Free Man said. They continued uphill.

The woods looked the same to Zack, but somehow felt different. The air seemed to thicken around him, as if he were walking through water. He felt lighter on his feet. While the ground became steeper, the going was easier. Craggy trees stood straight up from the sharply angled ground. The temperature rose. Snow and brittle leaves underfoot gave way to a soft carpet of mossy earth.

"What's going on?" Zack asked. His voice was muted, as if he were speaking through a pillow. The Free Man turned and nodded in what looked like slow motion.

"We are approaching Yggdrasil. The woods around it are heavily enchanted." His words seemed to hang in the air, like soft echoes.

Soon the ground was nothing but brilliant green moss. It reminded Zack of Astroturf, but much softer. "My dad would love this stuff in the house," he said without even thinking.

He quickly turned his head so the Free Man couldn't see his face. Every time Zack thought about his dad, he felt a rush of emotions that only made it harder for him to focus on what he had to do here in order to get back to him, to get back to everyone back home.

Again the ground leveled out. Zack saw a massive tree trunk looming deeper in the woods, dwarfing everything around it. It was as broad as any building in Minneapolis and stretched upward farther than Zack could see.

"That must be Yggdrasil."

"What you can see here is just a small part of it," the Free Man said. "Huginn and Muninn sometimes stop here on their way to and from Asgard."

Zack sighed with relief. Finally, they had arrived.

Before he could take another step, something tackled him from behind. Something big and heavy took him down, then charged past. Zack rolled over quickly and saw a huge, brown piglike animal turning around to face him. It was the size of a pony and had two curved tusks poking out from its round piggish snout. A long tuft of white hair ran along its head like a Mohawk.

It pawed the ground and shook its head, sending out a spray of slobber. The creature seemed intent on Zack, as if the Free Man wasn't even there.

"What is it?" Zack said, not taking his eyes off the beast.

The Free Man spoke in a hushed tone. "Hildisvini."

"Hildis . . . what?"

"A race of battle swine. They guard Yggdrasil everywhere.

You're going to have to get past him before we can continue."

Zack stood up slowly to a crouching position. "Can't you talk to him? Tell him why we're here."

"He knows why we're here. Battle swine are smarter than they look. I'm sure he can smell the key. To him, it smells of Yggdrasil."

Zack swallowed hard. The swine stood its ground between Zack and the tree. "What should I do?"

The Free Man sat down. "He is very stubborn. You will have to meet him on his own terms."

"His own terms? What are they?"

"Find a way to connect with him and find a way past him."

"Why are you just sitting there? Can't you help or something?"

The Free Man pointed to Zack's chest. "I'm not the one with the key. He'd kill me in a moment if I tried to go first."

Zack wanted to get mad but he sensed that the Free Man was right. The hildisvini seemed only to have eyes for him.

"Oh, and be careful of its tusks," the Free Man added. "They're quite poisonous."

"Fine," grumbled Zack, trying not to make any sudden moves.

Sure thing. Poison tusks. No problem.

He mulled over the Free Man's advice, repeating it in his head over and over.

Meet it on its own terms. Meet it on its own terms.

The battle swine calmly munched at the mossy ground.

Zack crouched down, slowly getting on all fours. He started crawling around, pretending to graze and trying to look as much like the battle swine as possible.

The hildisvini snorted, spraying more of its foamy spit. Zack reached into his shirt and held up the key. "Okay, nice piggy," he said, moving cautiously forward.

The swine charged. In a moment, it had covered several yards of ground. It plowed into Zack, knocking the wind out of him and leaving him, once again, flat on his back. Then it circled around to where it had been before and waited.

Zack stood up, trying to ignore the pain in his ribs. "Any ideas?"

The Free Man had been looking from Zack to the swine and back again, like a tennis match. He raised his eyebrows and shrugged. "Keep trying."

"Thanks. Thanks for the advice."

Zack turned his attention back to the task at hand. He looked around and found a scrubby bush with red berries on its branches. He broke off some stems and held them out as he moved toward the swine. "Mmm, leaves and berries, nice lunch. Here you go, big boy."

Again, the hildisvini charged. Zack dodged to the side, but the creature bodychecked him, catching him in the hip and spinning him to the ground. On its way back, it snatched the branch out of his hand. It chewed and swallowed noisily, waiting for Zack's next move.

Zack felt a stream of anger mixing in with his frustration. He had more sore spots than he could rub and he wasn't getting any closer to the big tree. The hildisvini seemed to sneer at him now.

With a sudden movement, Zack faked a charge, taking two steps forward and causing the swine to launch another attack. Again, he feinted to the side as the hildisvini was upon him. This time, he grabbed the animal in a headlock. Momentum carried them both forward. Zack was lifted off his feet. It was just a little bit like wrestling with his father, or one of his father's friends.

The hildsvini's legs tangled with Zack's and they stumbled. Zack still held on to the creature's neck and he pulled himself on top of its body as they rolled to a momentary stop. He straddled it like an upside-down horse. For a second, he seemed to have it immobilized but then the hildisvini screamed and bucked violently, rolling to the side and sending Zack down. It rolled over on top of Zack with a scramble of its sharp hooves. In a flash, their positions were reversed and now the hildisvini had Zack pinned underneath its considerable belly, which hung low to the ground. Its snout dripped onto Zack's face. Zack twisted his head to the side but couldn't move his body an inch.

The swine leaned in closer. It opened its mouth revealing a set of nubby teeth, with two sharp fangs in the front. Zack kept his head to the side—better to have his ear bitten off than his nose.

Something rough and wet scraped his cheek. The swine's tongue found the inside of Zack's ear and began lapping away. It tickled and Zack squirmed. The swine loosened his grip, and Zack crawled out from underneath it. Now it leaned down in a sort of bow with its front legs bent. Its curlicue of a tail wagged back and forth.

"Sometimes it takes the language of battle to make a friend," said the Free Man. "You speak battle swine very well."

Zack laughed out loud. The growling and snorting had been replaced with playful yipping and whining. He picked up a stick and threw it into the woods. The hildisvini charged after it and brought it back, dropping it at Zack's feet. The stick was shiny with a thick coat of saliva. Zack scratched between the swine's ears and it leaned into him for more.

"So can we go now?"

The hildisvini pranced along behind them as they moved on to the base of Yggdrasil.

"This is just part of it?" Zack asked. It was hard to imagine that the staggering tower jutting up out of the ground in front of them was only one branch in a larger tree. The first overhanging limb was at least two hundred feet above them, well over the tops of the other trees in the forest. The bark was craggy and rutted with wide trenches that ran up as far as Zack could see. Each one was big enough for Zack to stand inside.

"I feel like an ant," he said. "How do we even know if Huginn and Muninn are here?"

"I'm sure they have seen us coming," the Free Man said.

"When do you think they'll be here?"

The Free Man tilted his head back and looked up. "They are probably already here."

Zack's head dropped, his chin falling against his chest. "Please tell me they're coming down."

The Free Man sat down again and leaned against the tree. The hildisvini curled up next to him. "We'll be right here."

"These birds do have wings, right? Can't they—"

"They don't need you. You need them."

Zack looked up at the vertical wall of tree bark. "No way. There is no way I can . . . I mean, how do you even . . . How does anyone even . . . You know, I'm not too crazy about heights." He knew he was wasting his breath, but if he didn't keep talking he was going to have to start climbing.

"You'll find the bark is very soft," the Free Man said.

Finally, Zack stood silent, weighing his options. He could start climbing, risk breaking his neck, and hopefully get some answers about finding his way home. Or, he could walk away, go back to Lykill, and eat barley mush for the rest of his life.

With a quick exhale, he put his hand onto the bark of the tree. It was covered with dents and crevices that made natural handholds. It reminded Zack of a climbing wall, the ones that were so popular in Minneapolis. He had never tried one. Now he wished he had.

I can do this.

He stepped up and pulled himself a foot off the ground. *I think I can do this.*

"Good luck, Zack," the Free Man said.

I hope I can do this.

What if I can't do this?

He reached again, found another place for his foot and moved up. He repeated the motions several times, settling into a rhythm—reach up, grab on, bring up the opposite foot, reach with the other hand, step up with the other foot. After several minutes of climbing he let himself look down. The ground was disappointingly close. He could still easily make out the expression on the Free Man's face.

"I'm going, I'm going," he said, and focused upward. He tried to concentrate only on the bark of the tree and his next move.

Hand up, foot up, hand up, foot up.

After what seemed like more than an hour of climbing, the lightness he felt on the ground had faded. His legs ached with each rise. The bark had seemed soft at first but now it bit into his fingers. He had blisters on both palms from gripping the side of the tree. When he kicked a foot into place, he often banged his shin as well. It was starting to feel as if the tree were beating him up as much as the hildisvini had.

Slowly, he passed the other treetops and came out of the shade of the forest into bright sunlight. With nothing around him but open air, and an endless valley spread out below him, he felt even more vulnerable than before. A gust of cold wind blew up the mountainside and nearly sheared him off the side of the tree. He stood still, clinging to the trunk as hard as he could.

When the wind had passed, he looked up. The first tree limb was still well out of reach.

Don't look down, don't look down.

He looked down. His stomach swung like a hammock inside him. He was much higher than he had realized. The Free Man was just a tiny figure on the ground. Zack turned his face to the tree and shut his eyes tight trying to slow down his rapid-fire breathing.

He thought about his house in Minneapolis. He created a picture in his mind—he was at home in Minneapolis, sitting on the couch, eating a giant cheeseburger with fries and gravy.

Nice thick, hot, gravy. Fries not too crispy.

His empty stomach rumbled a complaint, but his heart and his breathing slowed down to something that felt almost normal. When he finally opened his eyes, it was hard to know how long he had been frozen in that position. He looked up and slowly reached for the next handhold.

He lifted himself up again, and again, and again. The repetitive motion dulled his brain. If he hadn't been in constant fear of falling, it might even have been boring.

Finally, the first tree limb loomed overhead. It was the size of a 747, jutting out from the side of the tree. It took Zack several more minutes of climbing alongside the limb before he could even see the top of it.

To stand on the limb, Zack had to traverse the tree, crossing sideways instead of up and down. He moved out of the groove where he had been climbing and reached over to the next one. It was like crossing from one ladder to another, with a wall in between the two.

He reached out, grabbed on with one hand, held his breath, and stepped across. His free arm swung wildly.

"No, no, no, no, no, NO, NO!" he shouted.

No falling. Not after all this.

His hand found a nub of bark and grabbed on. He knew he was starting to take chances. He would have to finish soon or he wasn't going to make it.

After crossing several more ridges, he was able to step down onto the limb. His hands felt stuck in a gripping position, like permanent claws. With a last push of concentration, he forced his fingers to let go and collapsed back onto semi-solid surface.

As he lay there, too tired to move, Zack felt a supreme sense of calm wash over him.

No one is ever going to believe this. I can't believe this. I wish Dad was here to see it. And Ollie. And Ashley. But mostly Dad.

For a few sweet moments, nothing else mattered.

A loud ruffling sound broke through Zack's thoughts. At first, all he saw were moving shadows. Then he realized the shadows were two enormous black birds. They fluttered down from a higher branch somewhere to land next to him. Each one was as large as Zack himself.

Zack sat up. "You must be—"

"Huginn," said one bird.

"And Muninn," said the other. Their tiny, high-pitched

voices didn't match their huge bodies at all.

"You are the Lost Boy," Muninn said. It wasn't a question.

"Let him speak," Huginn said.

"Let him speak," Muninn repeated, in a harsh mocking tone.

"There are things you will need to know," Huginn said.

"I thought we were to let him speak," Muninn interrupted.

The two birds started squabbling and ignored Zack altogether.

Zack took out the key and tried to speak over their arguing. "What can you tell me about this?"

Huginn abruptly turned to him. "There are three things we can tell you. The key brought you here—"

"I want to tell," Muninn snapped.

"Fine. Go ahead."

"One, the key brought you here. Two, the key will open Yggdrasil's Chest—"

"And three, the key must be returned," Huginn finished quickly.

Zack wasn't sure where to start. "Can the key get me back home again? Back where I came from?" he asked.

"Yes," Huginn said.

". . . and no," Muninn added. "The key may take you home and it may not. But that is not where it belongs."

"Is that what you meant when you said it has to be returned?" Zack asked.

"Yes," said Muninn.

". . . and no," Huginn said. "Listen carefully. This key is not something you keep. Just like you, it has a home."

"Do you mean Yggdrasil's Chest?"

"No," said Huginn.

"Well no, and yes," Muninn said. "The key and the chest belong together."

"But there is more to it than that," Huginn said. "It is up to you to know when the key must be surrendered."

Muninn jumped in. "It cannot be taken from you. The key must be given willingly. Perhaps you already know this."

Zack thought again about how Orn had flown through the air when he tried to take it. "Yeah, I've noticed. So, the key can be given but not taken?"

"Correct."

"How do I know when I'm supposed to give it up? Where's the key supposed to go?"

"When the time is right, you will know," Huginn said.

"I was just going to say that," Muninn said.

"But what about getting home? How do I get home?"

"Follow the prophecy," Muninn said. "It is the only way."

And then both birds began reciting the prophecy together, in a screeching singsong.

Zack waited patiently until they were done, with Huginn's "The Boy will lead until the end," finishing a second or so after Muninn's. "I've heard the prophecy, but what does 'the end' mean? Where am I supposed to be leading?"

"First to the chest," Huginn said. "You are looking for the

chest, and the Bears are looking for you."

"Do you know where the chest is?"

"It is always with the one called Erik the Horrible. He is never far from it," Muninn said.

"They have a camp—" Zack began.

"Not far from here," Huginn finished for him. "That is where the chest is."

"What should we do?" Zack asked.

"Act quickly," both birds said at once.

"And then what? What's in the chest? What do we do with it?"

"Yggdrasil's Chest holds great treasures," said Huginn.

"Yes and no," said Muninn. "Do not mislead him."

"Mislead him? I'm doing nothing of the sort." Again the birds began to squawk angrily at each other.

"You still haven't told me how to get home." Zack waited as they continued to fight, then repeated his words, louder this time.

"But we have," Muninn said.

"Follow the prophecy," Huginn added.

They began it again, in unison. "Yggdrasil's Chest, Yggdrasil's Key—"

"I know, I know," Zack said, holding up his hands. "I know the prophecy."

"Then you know all you need to know," said Huginn.

"On that I completely agree," said Muninn.

Zack slowly shook his head.

I'm going to be eating barley mush for the rest of my life. I'm never going to see another French fry again.

Muninn lifted his head and spread his wings. "It is time for us to go. We have many places to be."

"Wait!" Zack yelled.

"We have told you all you need to know," Muninn said.

"More than you need to know," Huginn added. "What else could you possibly need?"

Zack looked over the edge of the branch. The sun was sinking low. "I could use a ride down. It was a long climb to get here."

Huginn sighed. "Very well. Go ahead, Muninn."

"Me?" Muninn snapped. "Why should I be the one?"

"You're stronger."

"Oh, now I'm stronger. Yesterday—"

After another several minutes of arguing, Huginn reluctantly agreed to take Zack to the ground. He held onto the giant raven's legs as the bird descended slowly from the branch. Winter wind whistled in Zack's ears and stung his face. The slope of the mountain fell away and he could see almost straight down to the valley far below. The horizon where the sun was beginning to set seemed impossibly far away. The earthscape beneath him was covered in slanting golden light.

Zack had once ridden a roller coaster where his feet hung free and the cars were suspended from tracks above. Flying with Huginn felt almost the same, except that Huginn was grunting and panting with each flap of his wings.

"Are you going to be okay?" Zack called out.

"Don't. Speak." the raven groaned as they dropped quickly through the air.

Muninn shot by, flying free. "Having trouble, Huginn?"

Within a minute, Zack and Huginn had passed through the forest canopy. They swooped downward, circling Yggdrasil in wide arcs. When they approached the ground, Zack yelled out a thank you to Huginn and let go of the bird's thin legs. He fell several yards onto a cushion of mossy earth. As he rolled to a stop, he could faintly hear the ravens' voices somewhere above him.

"What are you doing? This way!"

"No, you follow me this time."

And then they were gone.

CHAPTER NINE

By the time they got back to the Free Man's cabin, it was well past dark. Olaf was waiting by the fire.

"Was good trip? Not too slow, Olaf not keeping you back this time?"

Zack shrugged at the troll and pointed to the Free Man. "Talk to this guy. He's the one who called the shots."

Olaf crossed his arms and turned away.

"We need to get back right away," Zack said. Olaf didn't speak. Zack was too tired to worry about it. He ate quickly and was asleep within minutes.

He woke in the middle of the next afternoon. Olaf sat at the table looking at him. His feet dangled from the human-sized bench, kicking back and forth in the air.

"Zack rested? Zack sleep enough? Zack not too busy to go with Olaf now?"

Zack sat up sluggishly, squinting at the daylight. "Zack hungry."

After a loaf of dark bread and two more bowls of the same gray stew, he was ready to go. The Free Man followed them outside and scanned the sky. When the white falcon passed over, he screeched up to it. The bird circled twice, then landed on the icy roof of the cabin. It had snow-white feathers from top to bottom. Its sharp claws gripped the ice as it called down to the Free Man.

"The path down the mountain is clear," reported the Free Man. "But beyond that, you should try to find another way back. Stay well clear of the Bear camp."

"Olaf know the way. Will travel carefully." Olaf looked at Zack. "Will not leave friend behind."

Wow. *Friend*. He'd kind of felt that way about Olaf since the first time he really saw him and realized the troll was the Viking version of Ollie, but it gave him a weird, kind of nice feeling to hear that Olaf felt the same about him. And Olaf was right—friends didn't leave friends behind. It hadn't been fair to leave Olaf behind, regardless of the Free Man's instructions. Zack wouldn't have left Ollie behind. And he wasn't going to do it to Olaf again, either.

After a brief thank-you and good-bye, they headed down the mountain. Zack kept his eyes up, scanning the woods and not just following blindly behind as he had done on the way out. The troll marched silently ahead, still grumbling to himself. Guilt trip or no guilt trip, it started to get old pretty quickly.

"Do you want to keep complaining, or do you want to hear about what happened?" Zack asked.

Olaf didn't turn around. "Zack can speak if Zack wants. Is not up to Olaf."

Zack told him all about the trip, and Huginn and Muninn, and what they had said. At first Olaf was silent but Zack recognized the way the troll's ears twitched when he was interested in something. Soon Olaf was asking questions, and by the time they reached the bottom of the mountain, things between them felt as comfortable as they had before.

Olaf veered off the trail and led Zack into the woods. Zack fought the impulse to ask Olaf if he knew where he was going.

"How long do you think it will take to get back?" he asked instead.

Olaf stopped at a stream, leaned over it, and sniffed the water several times. "Is maybe by dark today," he said. "This way go." They followed the water upstream for several hundred yards.

The first unusual thing Zack noticed was a slight vibration under his feet.

"Olaf?"

The troll had already stopped. "Yes. I feel."

Almost immediately, Zack heard the soft thudding of hooves. He turned around. Horses were moving in. Five of them wove through the woods at top speed, each mounted by a bearskin-clad soldier. There was nowhere to run, no time for a plan. Zack instinctively pulled out the only weapon he had—the key. He could only hope someone would try to take it from him.

As the first soldier lunged for them, Zack and Olaf leapt out of the way, in opposite directions. Two of the soldiers stopped short, turned their horses and closed in on Zack.

"Run!" he yelled. But Olaf stood his ground and even waved

his arms, trying to divert the Bears' attention to himself.

Zack paused, torn. His first impulse was to run toward Olaf, try to help him. He was furious at the troll for making himself a target like that. But in the same moment, Zack recognized what the sacrifice was about. It wasn't just for him but for the good of Jok's entire tribe, whose fate seemed to rest on Zack's shoulders. And it looked as though the only chance either of them had now was if Zack could get away. With a quick shake of his head, Zack took off again and leapt across the stream. Two horses followed. Somewhere behind him, he heard Olaf shouting and then right away felt the crushing weight of two bodies falling onto him from both sides.

One of the soldiers was on top of Zack, the other one beneath him. Zack used his body weight to heave the soldier off his back. The soldier slammed into a tree and Zack stood up. Two more Bears were charging toward him. He turned to run again but one of the Bears was still underfoot. Zack managed only a step before the Bear grabbed his ankle. He went down again. All of the other Bears piled on in a group tackle, leaving him pinned and helpless.

He struggled and kicked but they were four against one. By the time they were clear of him, his legs and wrists had been bound with rope. Poor Olaf had given himself up for nothing. When Zack looked down at his hands, he realized with a horrible sinking feeling that they were empty. The key was gone.

The soldiers yelled at him and one another, their words a garble. The language was a complete mystery to Zack's ears.

He looked wildly around for the key as they dragged him to his feet.

Do they have it? Did I drop it? Is it under the snow?

None of the soldiers seemed to be holding the key, which was only a small comfort given the current situation.

They secured a line between him and one of the horses, then untied his legs. He was going to have to follow behind. Zack was barely aware of what they were doing. He twisted his head, trying to look in every direction at once. If the key was on the ground, it could have easily been buried in snow, and just as invisible as when he had tripped over it in the Metrodome parking lot. Either way, it was gone—the key, the prophecy, the chest, and any hope of ever getting home again. A horrible sense of loss threatened to overwhelm him.

Focus, Gilman, focus.

He forced himself to look past his panic and keep searching the ground while he had the chance.

Olaf called out to him in an urgent tone but with words Zack couldn't understand. The troll was already tied up and had been put on the back of a horse behind one of the soldiers. The soldier turned toward Olaf, then laughed.

"I don't know what you're saying," Zack said, but he knew it was no use. Olaf looked back with a confused expression. There was no way to explain.

As they began to move out, Zack desperately tried to record the details of the setting.

Stream, tall pointed rock, fallen evergreen tree . . .

If he got away, he would try to come back here and look for the key. That was, assuming the Bears didn't already have it. That didn't seem possible, but it was even more impossible to know.

The rope jerked and pulled him forward as the horses headed out. It was all Zack could do to keep up. Olaf continued to shout things back at him, none of them understandable. The horses trotted through the woods and soon came into a familiar clearing. They were back at the Bear camp.

Zack looked over at Erik's tent with the red and black flags waving.

Is that where they have Yggdrasil's Chest?

Even if it was, Zack couldn't imagine any way of getting to it, much less stealing it away.

Two soldiers searched Zack, patting him down and reaching into his pockets. When they didn't find anything, they tied Zack and Olaf to two wooden posts on the edge of the camp, and then marched away.

Several other soldiers came over and leered at them from under their hoods. While Zack couldn't understand their words, he was pretty sure he didn't like what they were saying.

Olaf seemed to have figured out what was going on. He looked desperately at Zack's chest. Zack shook his head from side to side, the only answer he could give.

Several more soldiers appeared. They were followed by Erik, with his torch-topped staff, and then Orn, who carried a large hunting knife. Two of the soldiers carried a chest. It was a plain wooden box, with black metal bands along the edges. Its lid was divided into three pieces, each one with a separate lock.

Three locks. A three-pronged key.

Yggdrasil's Chest.

Zack was surprised at how ordinary the chest looked, like something you'd find at a thrift store. The wood was a dull brown and looked as if it had been beaten in several places with a hammer. He had expected something much more impressive. But this had to be it. The look on Olaf's face told him he was right.

The soldiers set the chest down behind Erik and stood on either side of it, hands on their swords.

Erik the Horrible strutted toward Zack with the same familiar Eric Spangler expression on his face. Zack imagined that the squint and the sneer were supposed to be cool and threatening, but it always looked to him more like Spangler was about to throw up.

Orn limped along behind Erik, sporting several new, mismatched toes on one foot. The new toes were the only part of him that wasn't hairy. They looked like little uncooked hot dogs, except for one, which was a sickly yellow color.

"I hope you didn't pay too much for those," Zack muttered. One of the Bear soldiers shouted something; probably for Zack to be quiet.

Erik sauntered slowly up to him. He whispered something in Zack's ear. Zack wanted to spit in his face, but he kept his temper.

Erik stepped back and repeated whatever he had said,

louder this time. Orn grunted and nodded his head. Zack hoped Erik was asking about the key. That would mean they had no idea where it was.

Erik tried again, his voice rising to a higher pitch. His eyes darted from side to side. He motioned to Orn and barked an order. Orn stood behind Olaf and held the knife to his face so Zack could see. He drew the knife slowly across Olaf's cheek. A streak of blood followed the blade but Olaf stood perfectly still.

Zack felt a surge of rage and panic inside him. He strained against the ropes. One of the soldiers shoved him painfully back against the post.

Erik repeated his question, pausing between each word.

"If I had it, do you think I'd be standing here, you dork?" Zack knew no one could understand him but it felt good to yell anyway.

Several of the soldiers began putting small pieces of wood and a pile of straw around Olaf's feet. Erik walked over to where Olaf was tied. Keeping his eyes on Zack the whole time, he carelessly waved his torch just above the wood and straw. He spoke casually, asking the same question once again.

Zack struggled and rocked against the post. It cracked— Zack heard a sharp snapping sound, but he was still tied firmly to it and couldn't move. Even if he could get free, he was completely outnumbered.

"I don't have it! Do you understand? I. Don't. Have. It."

How could he make them understand?

Erik turned on his heel and started giving orders. Zack looked at Olaf's bleeding face.

"I'm sorry," he said. "I'm sorry."

Olaf stared intently at Zack. He seemed to be trying to say something without words. His eyes darted toward the woods and back again. Zack followed his gaze and saw two enormous black shapes perched in the forest just past the tree line. Huginn and Muninn.

Erik turned back to Zack and began speaking again, while two soldiers untied the rope that held him to the post. His arms were still bound and two other soldiers held him in place.

Erik pointed to Olaf as he spoke. He held up two fingers and shook them at Zack, emphasizing . . . something. Then he turned again and walked quickly back toward his tent, followed by Orn and several others.

Someone slipped a sack over Zack's head. Zack felt several pairs of hands pushing him along and then lifting him onto a horse. The Bears strained to get him off the ground and Zack let himself go limp, not wanting to make it any easier. He felt more and more hands getting in on the job. Finally, they had him on horseback. Someone else mounted in front of him and they took off. With his hands tied, Zack had to hold tightly with his legs to keep from falling. He could hear at least two others cantering alongside.

He called out. "Olaf?" But there was no response. Olaf was still back at the camp.

The beating of hooves muted slightly as they passed into the forest. Which direction or where they were headed, Zack had no idea.

His mind spun. On top of everything else, he felt responsible for losing Olaf, maybe even costing Olaf his life. And who knew what was coming next? He imagined his own body thrown over a cliff to the rocks hundreds of feet below. He saw himself, bound and hooded, helpless, as wild animals made a live meal out of him.

Eventually, they came to a stop. The rider in front of Zack called out to the others. Someone reached over with a knife and cut the rope around his wrists. Before Zack could manage to remove the sack from his head, he was shoved to the ground. He landed with a painful wallop on his side as the soldiers galloped away. He pulled off the hood and found himself in the middle of nowhere. The woods looked just like everywhere else he had been. It all looked the same, but nothing was familiar.

Why did they let me go? And . . . where did they let me go? Where am I?

"Hello?!"

The spot where the Bears had first captured him could be any number of miles in any direction from where he now stood. Yet that's where he had to go. That was his best shot at finding the key again. But which way?

"Hello?!"

A welcome sound greeted his ears. Two great sets of wings flapped in the air above the trees. Huginn and Muninn—he could no longer tell which was which—descended to a branch over his head.

Zack let out a huge sigh of relief. "I am so glad to see you guys. Can you help me? I—"

The birds cawed. Their voices were bird voices. Their language, just like Olaf's, Erik's, and everyone else's, was gone to him now.

". . . lost the key," he finished quietly.

Without another sound, the birds lifted off and flew to a nearby tree. They looked at Zack and called out. One of them hopped on the branch, as if to say "hurry!"

Zack ran after them. They flew on and landed again. He followed along this way until they came to the familiar streambed. When he saw the tall pointed rock and the fallen evergreen, his heart leapt. He found hoofprints and followed them across the stream, to where the snow cover was most disturbed.

"This is where they got me," he told the ravens. He threw himself down on the ground, feeling through the ice and snow. A piece of leather caught his eye. Zack pounced on it and pulled. The strap came out of the snow, broken and empty.

"It's not here," he wailed. The birds cawed, clearly urging him to keep looking.

Zack combed the ground some more, his fingers growing numb in the snow. Then his hand hit metal. His stiff fingers closed around it and he lifted the key up in the air.

It was back.

"Thank you, thank you, thank you, thank you," he repeated.

"You are welcome," said Huginn.

Zack looked up to them with a laugh. "I can understand you!" And then his thoughts went right back to Olaf. "Do you know what they've done with Olaf? Is he still alive? What's going on?"

Muninn nodded. "Yes, he's alive. They are holding him until you return with the key."

"You were freed under certain conditions."

"We heard it all."

"What conditions?" Zack asked, his heart pounding.

"Erik thinks you have the key hidden back in the village. He said you were smarter than he thought, by not traveling with it."

"Smarter than him at least," Zack said.

"He said you are to bring the key to him. You are to meet him in the Ice Fields by mid-afternoon in two days."

Zack nodded, remembering Erik's two fingers shaking in his face. "Where are the Ice Fields?"

"In the north," Huginn said. "Your people will know how to find them."

Muninn spoke now. "He said if he doesn't have the key by then, Olaf will be burned."

"And he says you are to bring Asleif the *skald* girl as well. He says she belongs to him."

Zack's insides squirmed. He couldn't stand still anymore and started pacing. "No way. No way to all of it."

"That is what he said."

"Well he can kiss my—"

"You should return to your village," Huginn interrupted. "There is not much time."

"Can you . . . " Zack thought frantically. He started climbing to where Huginn and Muninn were perched. "Can you fly me there? Now?"

"Er . . . " said Huginn.

Muninn chimed in. "Perhaps you should follow behind. Huginn found you to be a bit much to carry."

"It's not that," Huginn said.

"Oh yes," Muninn said. "I keep forgetting how *strong* you are."

"Well perhaps you should carry him, then."

Muninn looked at Zack. "Follow us. Try to keep up."

Without another word, the birds took flight. Zack clutched the key against his chest and followed the ravens, running as fast as he could toward Lykill.

CHAPTER TEN

Jok paced in front of the fire. As Zack explained the situation, Jok's shoulders rose toward his ears. His hands were balled into fists and he punched at the air.

"The greedier Erik becomes, the more I want to squash him like a toad," Jok seethed. "It's not even his own power he uses. It's his father's. Erik the Rich pays for all this misery. But the son is the wretch who makes it happen."

Jok spread the word immediately. Their offensive against the Bears would be much sooner than they had planned. They were going to get Olaf. They were not going to give up the key. They were not going to give up Asleif. And they were not coming home without Yggdrasil's Chest.

Zack looked at the ground and didn't say much as everyone slapped him on the back and welcomed him home.

"I feel badly," he told Harald. "I'm here, all safe and taken care of, but Olaf's still out there."

"We'll get him back," Harald told him. "Don't worry. It's not your fault."

"It is my fault," Zack said. "If he hadn't been with me, this wouldn't have happened to him."

Clearly everyone else felt the absence of Olaf, too, because the evening feast was considerably more somber than the last one Zack had seen. The musicians played again, but Asleif did not sing and there was no celebration.

Zack watched carefully as Valdis loaded his plate with food.

"No 'spices' this time," he said.

"The magical orphan boy is somewhat particular, even when given the best of everything," Valdis said to another woman beside her as they served. She handed Zack his plate without looking at him.

Zack sat with Jok and his closest advisors while they ate and made plans.

"What if we do give them the key?" Zack asked. "If we have to. Isn't that worth it to save Olaf?"

"We are not giving up the key," Jok said evenly.

"But—"

"And we are *not* losing Olaf. He will ride Yggdrasil's Chest on the deck of the *Winniferd*, all the way home."

Everyone passed their drinking horns in a toast to what Jok had said. Valdis handed a horn to Zack, and before he thought about it, he drank with the others. He looked at Valdis but she seemed completely unaware of him.

Maybe there wasn't anything wrong with it. I didn't see her put anything in there.

A few minutes went by, and then the musicians stopped playing. Asleif set down her harp and stood up, stretching her fingers. Zack forced himself to stand up as well. This was going to be his moment. If he could climb hundreds of feet up a giant tree, and do everything else he had done in the past few days, he could at least say a few things to Asleif.

She seemed to know he had her in mind. She looked expectantly at him across the room.

Don't think about it. Just go.

Zack took a step toward her and his foot felt like it was on backward. His leg twisted under him and he stumbled. Asleif held a hand up to her mouth but her eyes betrayed the smile she was trying to hide. Zack forced a smile of his own, trying to play it off. He stood up straight again and tried another step. His brain thought "forward" but again his foot went backward. He bumped into the table and sat hard on a plate of mutton.

Everyone around him snickered. Lars grabbed whatever mutton wasn't trapped under Zack and put it on his own plate.

Before Zack could help it, his body twitched, and he flopped over the end of the table, pulling the whole thing down like a giant teeter-totter. Platters of food and buckets of ale went crashing, most of them right onto Zack. The longhouse was filled with shrieks of laughter.

He stood up and pointed at Valdis, only to have his arm flop out of control and poke himself painfully right in the eye. Everyone roared even louder.

"Valdis!" Jok erupted, above them all. "How many times have I told you—you are never, never to use that elixir again!" But even he seemed to be trying not to laugh as he scolded her.

Zack stumbled toward the door. All he wanted now was

to get out of there. His feet poked out in several directions like bad dance moves as he pushed through the laughing crowd. Finally, he made it outside and sat down. He leaned against the wall of the longhouse, wet, covered in food, and fuming.

The laughter inside got louder for a moment, and then quieter again as the door opened and closed. Zack felt the blood rising in his face as Asleif sat down next to him.

"She doesn't mean any harm," Asleif said. "I think she might be jealous of you."

"Jealous?" Zack almost choked on the word but he fought to keep his voice cool. He didn't want Asleif to think Valdis had gotten the best of him.

"I've seen how protective she can be with Jok," said Asleif. "Her mother disappeared nine years ago, and she's been his only family since."

"Winniferd," Zack said, half to himself. Every time someone mentioned her, Zack thought about the framed photo of his own mother next to his bed at home.

I'll bet they looked alike.

"Valdis doesn't let much come between her and her father," Asleif said.

"I've noticed," Zack said. So Asleif was both pretty *and* smart. Everything she said made sense.

A long silence stood between them. Zack felt a few twitches in his legs from Valdis's potion. He wrapped his arms around his knees.

"Do you think they're hurting him?" Asleif asked.

"Olaf?" Zack realized immediately how silly it was to be upset over Valdis's stupid prank when his friend was out there somewhere, held by someone as cruel as Erik the Horrible.

"Yes. When I was Erik's slave, I saw many terrible things."

Zack thought about it, trying not to imagine any of the scarier possibilities. "I think they'll keep him safe enough at least as long as they want the key," he said finally, hoping to reassure himself as well as Asleif.

"And me."

"What?"

"I know how he works," Asleif said. "He wants the key most of all. But he wants me returned to him, too, doesn't he?"

Zack started to lie but when he looked into her eyes, he couldn't. "Yes. That's what he said."

Asleif stood up. "Well, no matter. He can't have me."

"That's right," Zack said. "He can't."

"Are you coming back inside?"

Zack straightened his legs. They wobbled just slightly. "I'm going to sit here and wait a little bit."

"Valdis's potion doesn't last long." She smiled down at him.

Zack smiled and nodded to her as she let herself back in. Then he smiled to himself.

Not bad, Gilman. Five whole minutes without embarrassing yourself. Next time, we'll go for ten.

A moment later, the gentle music inside started up again. Zack listened, sitting on the cold ground but feeling as warm as if he were next to the fire.

⌒⌒

Zack bolted upright in bed. He thought the shouts had been part of his dream. They were coming from all over the village.

It was still dark out. The door to the longhouse stood open. He saw people with torches running past. A bonfire had been lit in the square outside Jok's gate.

Voices from all directions punctuated the confusion.

"Here they come!"

"There's another! Get out of the way!"

Zack was outside in a flash. The first person he recognized was Harald.

"Is it the Bears? Are they here?"

"Duck!" Harald yelled. He swung his torch wildly over Zack's head and connected with something just behind him. Zack turned and saw a dark figure go down. By the light of the nearby bonfire, he could make out its huge eyes and pointed snout. Its body was like that of a small man, but with birdlike claws at the end of each arm and leg.

"Hobgoblins!" Harald shouted. "Foul scavengers—they'll eat anything, including humans." He pressed his torch into Zack's hand. "Use your fire," Harald urged, and he ran off.

Zack spun around. He could hear, and vaguely see, trees all around the village shaking and alive as if they were filled with flocks of crazed birds. The air seethed with strange

143

squeals, like a cross between a rusty hinge and an angry cat. The sound made his skin crawl with goose bumps.

Everyone seemed to know what to do. Most people had a torch in one hand and a weapon of some sort in the other. Valdis ran past him into the longhouse and rushed back out with a bucket of tallow, which was used like oil for the indoor lamps. She sloshed some of it onto the bonfire and it blazed higher. The sudden explosion of light made Zack jump.

He caught sight of Jok in the yard. Hobgoblins were dropping to the ground around him like rotten fruit from a nearby tree. He kept them at bay with his torch and used his sword when they came within striking distance.

Stop waiting for instructions, Gilman—do something!

Zack ran into the yard and took a position next to Jok. His torch started swinging before he even knew what he was doing. With the extra firepower, Jok was able to work twice as quickly with his sword. They moved together, driving back several hobgoblins at once. Zack knew just when to swing and when to get out of the way.

As some of the beasts ran off, others moved in from the forest. Zack's heart still raced but his brain was working even faster.

"I've got an idea," he shouted. "You okay here?"

"Go!" Jok yelled.

Zack tore back into the house. Working as quickly as he could, he grabbed a bolt of the linen material Valdis used for bandages. He ran outside, where he saw Lars piling more wood onto the bonfire.

"Lars! Grab this!" he yelled, unfurling the cloth.

A small group of hobgoblins went racing by on all fours, followed by Sigurd, Asleif, and several other villagers, yelling and waving their torches. The hobgoblins ran a wide arc around the bonfire, giving Zack some space in which to work.

He and Lars laid the cloth out on the ground. Zack spread oily tallow over it and told Lars to find some rope. Lars was back in a moment with a length of cord. He helped Zack bind the corners of the sheet together. They lifted it up and held it with its loose opening as far over the fire as they could. The makeshift balloon quickly filled with hot air. Zack could feel the heat of the flames on his skin and held on for as long as he could.

"Lars," he shouted, "get an arrow ready." He had no idea if this was going to work but there was no time to wonder. They had one chance.

Lars seemed to understand. He dipped an arrow in what was left of the tallow and then lit it in the bonfire. Zack released the tarp and it rose several feet into the air, just clearing the village rooftops. That was all Zack needed.

"Now!"

Lars shot the flaming arrow straight into the tarp and it burst into flames with an explosion of light and heat.

All over camp, Zack heard hobgoblin squeals rise in pitch to a piercing scream. For a moment, the village was illuminated by the fireball. Zack saw dozens of hobgoblins all scampering like rats in the same direction, toward the woods.

He and Lars followed several of them into Jok's yard. Jok was still there, chasing them off now, in large numbers. Several hobgoblins retreated higher into the branches of the closest trees.

"That tree, now!" Zack called out, pointing to a tall, brittle evergreen, its few needles dead and brown.

Lars, Jok, and Zack set their torches to it, and the tree went up like a giant torch itself. Burning wood and ash fell to the snow below as the forest echoed with hobgoblins' screams. They leaped from one treetop to another, and then to the ground, racing off into the night.

Zack felt a broad smile cross his face as Lars wrapped an arm around his neck. Jok shoved in, too, belly first.

"The vermin won't soon be back!" he yelled.

They walked out to the square, where people were jumping and cheering. Zack plunged giddily into the middle of them all.

"How did you know that would work?" Harald yelled in his ear.

"I didn't!" Zack answered. They both laughed as if it was the funniest thing they had ever heard.

"Zack the unbeatable!" Jok shouted.

"Zack the unbeatable!" everyone yelled back.

Zack leapt up on a bench next to the fire, raised two fists in the air, and shouted.

"V–I–K–I–N–G–S!"

And everyone shouted with him in response, "Go, Vikings, let's go!"

Even as he was doing it, Zack knew that standing on a bench and cheering like—well, like his father—was the last thing he would ever have done back home. Jock Gilman would have loved every second of this, too. Not only was Zack showing a little fire in the belly, as Jock always called it, but he was acting like a chip off the old three-hundred-pound block. And it felt good. It wasn't embarrassing at all. This must have been what Jock meant when he talked about Minnesota Vikings purple pride. Standing in front of all those people, Zack was as proud as he had ever been. It was a rock star moment and he just let himself soak it up.

Before long, the celebration died down and people began filtering back to their houses.

"Time for some more sleep," Lars said with a stretch.

"Shouldn't we keep a guard or something?" Zack asked. "What if they come back?"

"Not to worry," said Sven. "Those things are an infernal nuisance, but nothing to stay awake over."

Zack was stunned, but from all the sleepy faces he could tell that he was the only one who felt that way.

As they headed inside, Jok grasped Zack's wrist and lower arm with both hands. "You honor us, Lost Boy. A place in Valhalla waits for you."

"Thanks, Jok," Zack said. "We did pretty well together, right?"

"As if we were one," Jok said. "As if you were my own son."

Zack half-smiled. What a strange mix of feelings. Jok was the closest thing Zack had to a father in this place. But he was also more like a friend, which was something his real father would probably never be. Jock Gilman always seemed to want Zack to change. Jok seemed to admire him just as he was.

How could this place be making him miss his father and see his faults at the same time? As hard as it was living here—no heat, no electricity, no pizza—some things were strangely easier. It was like he was splitting down the middle, turning into two Zacks. One of him wanted more than anything to get home and see his dad. The other was beginning to see that there were some things he'd miss when—or if—he ever got out of here.

CHAPTER ELEVEN

The next morning, plans began in earnest for Olaf's rescue and the recovery of the chest. Smoke belched from Jok's forge. The yard echoed with the pounding of hammer against blade, as Jok and Sigurd worked quickly to sharpen and repair as much of their arsenal as possible.

Zack helped carry provisions to the beach, where the *Winniferd* was loaded with barrels of water and great sides of dried meat. Other men were busy pounding nails to reinforce the hull and mast of the ship.

Sven stood near the prow, pointing and shouting orders. "This should be a quick trip," he told Zack, "if we're lucky. But it's best to be prepared. There was a raid once, not too many years ago. We set out with nothing more than a skin of ale to our names. . . ."

Zack kept moving. The busier he stayed, the less time he had for worrying. His free moments were filled with thoughts of Olaf. He kept seeing Erik's torch playing around Olaf's feet, threatening to burn him. Erik seemed like the torturing type. Burning, hot oil, beating. Who knew what he was capable of?

We're coming, Olaf. Just hang on.

He heaved a barrel up to one of the men already on board

and jogged over to where Lars was stirring a cauldron of thick black tar. Lars handed him a pair of tongs. They worked together, dipping fist-sized balls of wool into the bubbling tar and plastering them to the sides of the ship.

"The less water we let on, the less bailing we have to do, the more hands we have for rowing," he explained.

"How soon can we go?" Zack asked.

"By sunrise tomorrow." Lars said.

That evening, Jok and the rest of the tribe reconvened at his longhouse to agree upon a plan of attack.

Valdis was not serving. She sat nearby, already eating, but Zack still wasn't going to take any chances. He helped himself to portions of boiled beef only after he saw Jok eating from the same pot. He filled a drinking horn from a barrel that Harald had brought from his house.

"I say we go in with one push, take out as many Bears as we can, and take our chances!" said one man.

"Take back Yggdrasil's Chest or die trying!" another man chimed in.

Zack stood up. "We need to think about this. We're completely outnumbered. I saw at least a hundred of them at that camp."

"Not completely outnumbered," Jok said. "We convene with Hilda and Helga at sea. Word has already come back from their village. They will join us."

"But even still," Zack pressed. "They're not going to let you just walk up and take the chest and Olaf. And what about Asleif? Erik made her part of the conditions, too."

"Asleif stays here," Jok said. "Erik's conditions are his own. This mission runs on my terms."

Zack tried to protest. "Yeah, how do you plan on—"

"Lost Boy," Sven interrupted, "we are honored by your presence, but even you must abide by our laws. No tribe member may participate in a planning council until he has proven himself in battle."

"I'm afraid that is true, Lost Boy," Jok said.

"Prove myself?" Zack said. "What about the hobgoblins?"

"What about them?" said Valdis. "Lost Boy, you don't think the disposal of a few vermin counts here, do you?"

Apparently, defeating hobgoblins was just pest control in this place.

"I'm sorry, Zack," Jok said. "You served us well last night. However, this is another matter."

"But—"

"Forgive me, Lost Boy," Valdis cut him off with a sneer, "but isn't it your doing that Olaf is gone from us to begin with? Getting back Yggdrasil's Chest was going to be difficult enough. Now it will be even harder."

"This is not Zack's fault," Jok said. Several others nodded in agreement.

Zack stared at Valdis. He wanted to defend himself but he couldn't. He felt responsible for Olaf's capture, whether they blamed him or not. He wondered if Olaf was still tied to that post in Erik's camp, and the thought of it pushed away anything he might have said. Silence filled the room.

"Our way is clear then," Jok said finally. "We will meet the

Bears at the Ice Field head on. We'll advance in pig-snout formation. We will hear their terms. And when the time is right, we will take them quickly by force. When we have Olaf and the chest, we reverse course and sail home. We will take no prisoners. Any questions?"

No one spoke.

"Good then," Jok said. "Get some sleep."

☙

The *Winniferd*'s yellow and white sail flapped in an early morning breeze. It cast a wide shadow over the ship, catching the first rays of sunrise on the horizon.

"Save your strength while you can, boys!" Jok shouted. "We'll row if we have to, but this morning we sail."

They rode the wind away from Lykill and up the fjord, winding their way toward broader waterways. By the time the sun was halfway toward overhead, the green and gold stripe of Hilda and Helga's sail came into view. Jok pulled up alongside their ship. Hilda and Helga's tribe was richly outfitted. Most of the warriors, men and women, wore silver chain mail and finely etched helmets.

Seated in the rear of the twins' ship was Asleif. Zack's jaw dropped open when he saw her. She waved somberly as the two ships pulled alongside each other. When her eyes met Zack's, she smiled and rose to her feet.

"What are you doing here?" Jok called out to her. "You were to stay home in the village."

"Erik asked for me as part of the deal," Asleif replied. "So he will think he's getting me—but just let him try to do it.

He'll see once and for all that I no longer belong to him. I learned a thing or two about defending myself when I was in his vile care." She held up a hammer she had been holding in the folds of her cloak. All the men and women cheered. Jok shook his head but he was smiling.

"She has been safe," Hilda said.

"I knew you would never let me sail with you," Asleif replied. "So I stole over to Hilda and Helga's village. Valdis knew where I was."

"We should sail on," Hilda said. "Move quickly."

Asleif climbed onto the ship rail. "Wait!" She stepped over to Jok's ship and jumped to the deck. "I will sail with my tribe," she proclaimed, looking straight at Zack.

Zack's heart thudded. He coughed and looked at the ground. Sven chortled and clipped him on the shoulder. Asleif worked her way to the back of the ship where she sat down next to him. Jok and Hilda both called for the sails to be snapped to, and they glided on northward.

"What are you doing here?" Zack asked her. "I can't believe you came."

"Erik has done many terrible things. I want to be there when he falls."

"Thanks," Zack said quietly.

"Thanks for what?" Asleif asked, looking under his downward cast face.

"For coming over here," he said. "You kind of surprised me. Actually, you really surprised me. You're not . . . exactly like I thought you were." Their eyes met.

"Good," Asleif said. "I'd hate to always be exactly what people think I am."

As the ships moved north, the stony mountains diminished to lower hills. The rich forest dwindled down to scrub and then to a barren nothingness, as if the earth here would not support living things.

"I can see why they call it the Ice Fields," Zack said.

"Some call this place the Hands of Death," Asleif said. "Nothing lives here. It is one long, inhospitable strip of land after another."

"Like fingers," Zack said. They were sailing along a narrow peninsula. Zack could see water on the far side and another icy finger of land beyond.

Asleif shivered. "People don't often come this way. Those who do don't always come back."

The wind continued to push them along, more slowly than before. Without rowing to keep them busy, most of the tribe settled into an ominous quiet as the ship coasted slowly along. Zack stamped his feet to keep warm—and to fight off his anxiety.

"There!" Sven called. On the other side of the peninsula, the sail of another ship could be seen, half black and half red. Jok called out to Hilda and Helga, and both ships angled in toward shore.

The peninsula was sloped on either side, with an expanse of flat ground in between. Zack couldn't see Erik's ship anymore. They would have to climb up the slope to know exactly where he was.

"Do you think they saw us coming?" Zack asked.

"I'm sure of it," Sven said. He called out to the others and everyone began unloading. Both tribes convened on the beach. Jok, Hilda, and Helga stood halfway up the slope and faced everyone else.

Jok spoke first. "We'll move up quickly and let them know we are here. If the moment is right, we charge. Stay close, stay strong. Watch for Yggdrasil's Chest, wherever it may be. With Thor's blessing, we'll have the chest by nightfall, and our friend Olaf as well." At that, the soldiers all beat their shields and cheered.

Hilda stepped up. "Watch the Lost Boy. Watch Asleif," she said. "Allow no harm to come to either of them."

Zack and Asleif stood in the middle of the crowd. Several of the tribe jostled them good-naturedly.

Lars put a helmet on Zack's head. "Don't worry, Lost Boy, we'll have the two of you home for a feast tonight."

"The three of us," Zack said. Himself, Asleif, and Olaf.

CHAPTER TWELVE

The tribes marched up the slope in a tight triangular formation with Zack and Asleif out of sight in the rear. As they came to a stop on flat ground, Zack could barely see over all the helmeted heads in front of him.

"What's going on up there?" Asleif asked.

Zack grabbed Asleif's hand and they pushed their way toward the front.

The Bears were also tightly clustered on the opposite side of the icy field. Behind them was the mast of their ship, sail lowered, and a lone red and black banner waving over their heads. Zack also saw that Erik's ship had a carving on the prow, in the same place as the dragonhead on the *Winniferd*. It was a skull, engulfed in flames. The skull's face was hollow-eyed and open-mouthed, as if frozen in a scream.

Zack scanned the crowd of Bears soldiers. With their hoods up, it was hard to tell one soldier from another. Erik and Orn, however, were nowhere in sight.

Then the Bears parted in the middle, stepping out of the way to reveal Erik standing in the rear, with Yggdrasil's Chest at his feet. Beside him was Orn, who held Olaf by the arm. Olaf's hands were still bound. His head was bowed and he looked as if he was having trouble staying on his feet.

The sight of Olaf chased Zack's nervousness right out of him. His breathing grew shallow and his heart started thumping out an angry rhythm. "I hate to think what they've been doing to him," he said bitterly.

"Nothing compared to what we'll do to them," Helga said.

Several of Jok's tribe surged forward at the sight of Olaf and the chest. Jok held up a hand and they stopped again.

"We've come for what's ours!" Jok bellowed.

Erik stepped forward, followed by Orn, Olaf, and five other Bear soldiers. The chest remained behind.

Jok leaned close to Hilda and Helga. They spoke in hushed tones for a minute and nodded their heads.

"What are they saying?" Zack asked.

Asleif squinted in their direction. "I don't know."

Jok, Hilda, and Helga came over. Hilda pointed to three others of their tribe who stepped out and joined them. Jok put a hand on Zack's shoulder.

"Follow along," Jok said.

"What?" Zack blinked. "What's going on? I thought—"

"Change of plans," Jok said. "Just follow along and do as Erik asks."

"What do you mean? This isn't what you talked about at all," Zack sputtered.

"We've had another thought," Jok said. "Trust me."

This was crazy. Even if Zack didn't agree with the battle plan they had made the day before, it was better than not knowing the plan at all.

"You've got to know the plays."

His father's voice came to him, like a vague echo. Jock had said it a million times. It never meant much to Zack. Now as he followed blindly along, it seemed like the truest thing in the world.

Jok, Zack, Hilda, Helga, and the others walked out to meet Erik's party at midfield. Their feet crunched across snow and ice in the otherwise silent air. Zack tried to make eye contact with Olaf, but the troll's head was bowed as he stumbled along at Orn's side.

"We're coming Olaf, we're coming," Zack muttered between clenched teeth.

When they were within several yards of each other, Erik stopped short. "That's far enough."

Orn moved Olaf in front of him like a shield. He seemed to use his mismatched arms fairly well. Keeping a tight grip on Olaf with one hand, Orn held up a short sword with the other and pressed it against Olaf's chest. Zack saw bruises on Olaf's face. One eye was swollen shut. Zack's hands closed into tight fists.

"I'll have the key," Erik said.

Jok nodded to Zack. Zack took the key out of his shirt but left it around his neck for the time being.

"How do you propose to have it?" Helga said.

"I propose," Erik said, raising his voice, "that the Lost Boy come forward, alone, and that he hand it to me of his own free will."

"What about Olaf?" Zack demanded.

"What about him?" Erik replied.

"You know what about him, you idiot."

"I'll ignore that comment for now," Erik said. He looked over at Olaf, as if he had just realized Olaf was there. "When I have the key, you'll have him back."

"Not good enough," Hilda said.

Jok pointed his sword at Orn. "Tell that one to put down his weapon."

"Do it," Erik commanded. Orn looked at Erik but didn't move. Erik repeated himself, speaking low and slowly. "I said, do it."

Orn tightened his grip on Olaf as he dropped his sword to the hard ground.

Jok turned to Zack. "Go ahead."

"Are you serious?" Zack whispered.

Jok nodded. "This is the only way to do it."

"All right then," Erik said impatiently. "Let's get this done with."

Zack turned and stepped forward. This was unbelievable. Jok had to have something up his sleeve. But giving up the key this way seemed like a huge risk.

He came face-to-face to with Erik. Slowly, he took the key from around his neck. They locked eyes. Erik reached out his hand.

"Be careful," Orn said suddenly. "The key can . . . be treacherous."

Erik froze. "You're right," he said, eyeing Zack suspiciously. Then he turned to Orn. "You do it."

"Me?" Orn whined.

"Yes," Erik said, taking a step back. "Good idea. Go ahead. Take the key and give them the troll."

Zack stood waiting with the key held out in front of him. "Do you want it or not?"

Orn inched forward, now using his backward-facing arm to pull Olaf along. He reached out tentatively with the other hand, his fingers trembling. He obviously didn't want to come any closer than he had to. Zack stood firm, ready to grab Olaf.

Orn shut his eyes and reached out as far as he could to wrap his hairy fingers around one of the key's stems. He gripped it lightly.

Nothing happened. No jolt of electricity. Orn was still standing. When he opened his eyes, he looked down at the key and then up at Zack. His mouth curled into a grin and he snarled.

Something rushed through the air between them. Zack caught sight of Jok's axe just as it flipped end over end and sliced Orn's arm off at the shoulder. Suddenly, the key came free in Zack's hand. Orn's long hairy arm came with it.

"Take that, you vermin!" Jok screamed.

Orn screamed, too. "My good arm!" He reeled, letting go of Olaf. Zack caught the troll before he slumped to the ground, and just before everything went crazy.

Orn went running. The Bear soldiers surrounded Erik. Hilda, Helga, and Jok started swinging. The field was instantly filled with the sounds of battle as both sides rushed toward each other.

It took Zack no time to pull Olaf back toward the *Winniferd*, running upstream against his own oncoming tribe. They weren't nearly in the clear yet, but Olaf was alive. That's what mattered right now. The troll stumbled and dragged his feet, but kept moving.

"I've got you," he yelled to Olaf. "Keep going."

"No choice," he heard Olaf mumble.

Asleif and Sven were waiting for him at the edge of the field. They carried Olaf down the slope toward the ship. They had to shout to hear each other over the sounds of the fighting up above.

"Olaf, are you all right?" Asleif yelled. She took off her cloak and they laid him out on the ground. Besides his bruises and swollen eye, he had large welts on his arms and legs.

"Olaf always all right," the troll said. He blinked twice and smiled up at them weakly.

"Glad to see you're still in one piece," Sven said.

Zack held up the key to show Olaf. "Which is more than Orn can say." Somewhere in their dash for the shore, the arm had dropped off. Just as well. That was one souvenir Zack could do without.

"Get ready to sail!" Hilda shouted down to them. Zack turned and looked up the slope where she was standing. Her chain mail was ripped down the middle. Her shield was stained with red. "When we need to go, we will need to go quickly!"

Sven carried Olaf toward the *Winniferd*. Asleif jumped onto Hilda's ship.

Zack put the key around his neck again and ran toward the field. "I'll be back!"

"Wait!" he heard Asleif yell, but he kept going. He had to keep going. This wasn't done yet.

"What can I do?" he shouted in Hilda's ear.

"Stay back!" she said. "There are too many of them. We're going to have to leave without the chest." She pointed across the field.

He could see an arc of Bear soldiers on the far side. Behind them was Yggdrasil's Chest. They had moved it back toward their ship but must have stopped to fight. The chest lay on its side behind them, as they clashed with Helga and several others. Erik cowered behind the wall of Bear soldiers, trying to drag the chest toward the ship by himself.

Closer by, Jok had retrieved his axe and was leading a group against a knot of Bear soldiers. One of the Bears lifted another of his own tribe members off the ground and used the body for protection, hurtling toward Jok. Jok squatted and tackled the oncoming pair, catching the first one in the legs and flipping both into the air.

Zack's entire system was charged with energy. With everything there was to see, he found his eyes drawn back to the chest again and again. Erik was making poor progress, but if they were going to get the chest, it had to be soon. Maybe the chest held answers for him and maybe it didn't. There was only one way to find out.

Suddenly, Jok was at his side.

"What are you doing up here?" he shouted. "Get back to the ship and stay there!"

"We need to get the chest!" Zack yelled.

"Maybe not today," Hilda said.

"They're too tight around it," Jok said. "Our formation has already broken up."

But Zack wasn't listening. He was remembering something. Something he never would have guessed might stay with him, even if he had heard it a million times.

"The Gilman Spread!" he shouted. Jock Gilman's favorite play. It was as if his father's voice had echoed through time, bounced off Zack's brain, and come out his mouth.

"What?" Jok yelled.

"Get seven others over here, right now," Zack said.

"There's no time," Jok said. "We have to pull out."

"Succeed or die trying!" Zack yelled. "Isn't that what you've always said?"

Jok and Hilda exchanged a glance. "This is our best chance," Hilda said.

"Go!" Zack yelled, and Jok was gone.

Less than a minute later, they were all huddled around Zack—Jok, Hilda, Helga, Sigurd, Lars, Harald, and two others. The battle raged all around.

Zack felt an odd sense of calm. It wasn't about knowing whether or not this would work. It was just a matter of knowing clearly what to try, what to do next.

"Okay, here's the chest, right? And they've got men all

around here and here." He drew a diagram in the snow with his finger. "Hilda, Helga, Sigurd, Lars, you, and you." Zack pointed to the Vikings he didn't know. "I need you to rush straight toward them shoulder-to-shoulder. Got it?"

Everyone shouted yes. Sigurd nodded vigorously.

"Jok, Harald, and I will be running just behind you guys," Zack continued. "When I give the signal, I want you to run through the middle, Harald. Make sure they see you coming; you're going to have to distract them."

Harald grunted his understanding.

"Then the backside guard and tackle have to pull toward the play side and lead block for me and Jok, while we run to get the chest. Okay, let's do it! Succeed or die trying, right?"

Silence. No shouts or battle cries. Just eight blank faces.

Zack frowned, confused, and then it hit him. He laughed. For once, he was the one who knew the most about football. "Uh . . . what I meant was that Hilda and Helga need to run towards the right to block for me and Jok so that we can sweep around the corner and grab the chest."

"Well then, why didn't you just say so?" Jok asked. "Succeed or die trying!"

They turned their attention to the field.

"Ready?" Zack shouted. "Go, go, go!"

With a roar and a rush of feet, they sped onto the field. "Stay tight," Zack shouted.

They rushed past dozens of soldiers, most of them locked in combat. Lars, Sigurd, and the rest of the human wall swung hammers and swords, keeping a berth of space around them as they made their way toward the far end.

The last barrier of Bear soldiers, with Erik and the chest beyond, grew closer. Zack's team let out a collective shout as they closed in. Several of the Bears turned their way, weapons raised.

With no more than ten yards to go, Zack waved his arms and shouted at the top of his lungs. "Now!" It was like flipping a switch, setting everything into motion.

Harald burst through the middle of the line, swinging his sword and roaring like, well, a big Viking warrior. Immediately, a large group of Bears ran toward him. For a second, Zack feared they would overwhelm Harald, but other Vikings came to his aid and it looked like the situation was under control.

Hilda and Helga dashed to the right, followed closely by Zack and Jok. The twins quickly engaged two of the Bears, thrusting, slashing, and parrying with astonishing speed and skill.

Four Bears remained between Zack and Jok, and the chest.

"Straight through!" Zack yelled. As one unit, he and Jok barreled their collective five hundred and fifty pounds into the group and, with a tremendous crunch of bodies, powered through them. Bears careened off Zack's shoulders with a painful crunch. But the pain was almost like fuel now. There was no stopping him.

Zack fell through, tumbling forward, flipping over and scrambling right back onto his feet. The chest, and Erik, were only a few strides away. He kept going. An animal growl boiled up from his stomach, worked its way past his chest and lungs, and exploded out his throat.

Erik's eyes grew wide. He made one last desperate tug on the chest.

"No!"

Zack tackled him for all he was worth. Erik's body left the ground as he flew back, his arms swinging helplessly in the air. When his feet hit the ground again, they took him backward and over the lip of the hill down to the shore.

Zack watched him roll out of sight in a blur of red cloth and spinning arms. He took a step to follow, but Jok clapped a hand on his shoulder.

"Forget him!"

Zack knew what they had to do. Erik had only gotten the smallest taste of what he deserved, but it was time to go. Right now, the chest was what mattered. It lay waiting for them in the snow. Jok waved to the others, pointing back toward the *Winniferd*.

Before any of the Bears had a chance, Jok and Zack each grabbed a handle on the side of the chest. Everyone closed around them and they headed back up the field.

"Go, go, go, go!" Zack yelled. The chest was surprisingly heavy but with the adrenaline rushing through him, it might as well have been made of paper. He ran faster than he ever knew he could.

Like a snowball rolling downhill, their small offense picked up other tribe members and grew larger as they ran. Soon, Zack and Jok were in the middle of a tightly packed arrow-shaped formation, barreling up the field. Zack could feel the key thumping against his chest. And he could feel his heart thumping, too, harder and harder as they neared the yellow and white of the *Winniferd*'s sail. The sail was fully raised and seemed to be waving them on.

Bears flung themselves at the tribe but were repelled with sword and spear and brute force. When Zack and the others tore down the hill to the beach, both ships were ready to go. Sven and Asleif stood on the decks and began firing arrows to repel the remaining Bears. The two tribes peeled off to their respective ships. Some leapt on board while others began pushing the ships off the beach and out of the shallowest water. A large group turned and faced the Bears, who were significantly fewer in number now.

Zack and Jok headed straight for the *Winniferd*. Without speaking, it was clear that Yggdrasil's Chest had to be secured above all else. Jok shouldered it as Zack climbed up to the deck. He and Sven took it from Jok and set it down between them. Once it was secure, Lars blew another blast on his horn, calling in the last of the troops. The remaining fighters worked their way backward, climbing onto the ship while those already on deck swung at Bears from overhead.

Sven called out aboard the *Winniferd* and Hilda did the same from the other ship, setting the rowers in motion.

"And . . . hoahhh . . . and . . . hoahhh."

Zack grabbed an oar and fell into rhythm with the others. The ship was already moving as the last of the tribe climbed on board to safety, leaving only a few ragged Bear soldiers standing along the shore.

CHAPTER THIRTEEN

"Look sharp, we're not out of it yet," Jok called. Their diamond-patterned sail sagged in the light breeze. The wind had been at their backs on the way north. Getting home would require more work. Sven called a steady rhythm as everyone settled to their oars. Zack gave his oar up to Sigurd, who had been one of the last fighters on shore. Sigurd nodded mutely to him as he took Zack's place. He almost looked excited, but as always, it was hard to tell.

"Erik would have to sail a mile up and a mile back to get around the finger," Sven said between calls. "We're safe from him, but its best to keep moving." Celebration would have to wait until later.

Zack's shoulders ached; his head throbbed from knocking helmets with at least one Bear soldier; he had a knot on his skull the size of a golf ball; his legs felt like rubber; his fingers were frozen; and he had a windburn on his face. He didn't feel any of it. He just saw the instant replay that ran like a loop, over and over, in his head.

Gilman bursts through for the tackle . . . and Erik goes down! Erik goes down! Erik goes down!

Yggdrasil's Chest had been recovered. Olaf was already bouncing back. The only thing Zack wished was to have

Asleif on board the *Winniferd*. She had readied Hilda and Helga's ship during the battle and was now sailing back with them. Zack heard Hilda calling out to her own rowers, in unison with Sven. He looked across the water. Asleif was at the ship rail, looking back. Even from more than fifty yards, her smile made him blush.

Olaf stepped up next to Zack and waved to Asleif. One of his eyes was still swollen shut, but he was already moving around the ship as nimbly as ever. Asleif blew him a kiss.

"Are you . . . blushing?" Zack asked. The troll's gray cheeks were turning a pale blue.

"No," Olaf said. "Is just happy. Is happy to see tribe again."

"I'm just glad we got to you in time," Zack said.

"Was no problem," said Olaf. "Olaf was soon to escape, was soon to rescue Yggdrasil's Chest himself."

Zack nodded. "Well, I'm glad we could help."

The chest sat nearby on the deck. Zack looked at it closely for the first time. It was about four feet long and as tall as Zack's knees. He looked at the strange lid of the chest, cut into three separate sections. On top of each section was an iron plate inscribed with a single word. He read each one out loud.

"Faith. Courage. Sacrifice." He looked at Jok. "Those are mentioned in the prophecy."

"They are what guide us," Jok said. "They are what make us who we are."

The wood and iron fixtures on the chest were heavily dented.

169

Each of the three locks had deep scratches and scrape marks all over.

"I really thought this was going to be made of gold or something," Zack said. "It looks so beaten up."

Jok put a hand on the lid. "You can see how many have tried to open it. There is no sword or hammer, or even fire, strong enough."

"Just this," Zack said, pointing to the key, and Jok nodded gravely. "What do you think is inside?"

"Our future," Jok said. "Our glory. And, with any luck, the end of Erik's power. Whatever treasure is in there, it has a powerful magic."

Zack looked down at the key, then at the chest, then back up at Jok. The temptation to open the chest right away was strong.

"Wait until we are home safe," Jok said. "Let everyone enjoy it when it happens."

Zack nodded. It made perfect sense to wait. Everyone in the village would want to be there when the chest was opened. But waiting was torture.

⤙⤚

Hilda and Helga followed the *Winniferd* to Lykill. As soon as the ships came into sight of the village, people started gathering around the dock.

Olaf stood up at the prow of the ship and waved. Behind him, Jok lifted the chest over his head. When he did, the crowd on shore began cheering and hugging one another.

"Is Olaf come home!" Olaf shouted, his voice too small to

be heard all that way. "Is happy to see everyone, too!"

Someone had brought a yellow and white banner and began waving it. Zack spotted Valdis and even she looked to be smiling and cheering along with everyone else. The villagers gathered around the ship as it came to a stop. Children were jumping up and down to get a better view. It was a similar feeling as the first time Zack had sailed into this bay. This time, however, it was all familiar—and just a little bit like coming home.

"Wait!" Jok yelled above the crowd. Everyone grew still. Jok motioned for Zack to come stand next to him.

"Yggdrasil's Chest," he said, "Yggdrasil's Key." Zack held up the key. "And Lost Boy will unite as three!"

That was all it took. The villagers went berserk. Everyone began hugging and kissing and shouting all over again. As they came off the ship, Zack and Jok were lifted above the crowd. A dozen or more people carried each of them into the village.

"It's all right," Zack tried to say. "I can walk if you want. . . ." No one was listening. They seemed intent on getting him all the way to the village square before setting him down.

The chest was placed on a table, where everyone gathered around. Jok stepped back and indicated that Zack should come forward. The festive mood was suddenly replaced by a quiet sense of anticipation.

Jok went down on one knee and everyone followed suit. Zack went down, too. It wasn't clear what was coming next.

Jok cleared his throat. "The key, Lost Boy," he said.

"Oh yeah," Zack said, putting a hand on the key and standing up again. The excitement made it easy to forget—they were waiting for him.

Jok spoke from where he kneeled. His words came slowly. "A circle is closed today, one that we always knew would complete itself, whether in our lifetime or in another. What we did not know, Zack, Lost Boy, is that you would become one of our own. We are proud to call you a son of the tribe."

Zack pressed his lips together in an embarrassed smile. Everyone was looking at him with solemn admiration. It didn't matter to them that practically no one in his high school knew who he was. It didn't matter that he was the underling who always had to make the bratwurst runs at the football games he didn't even want to go to in the first place. It didn't matter that he wasn't the star athlete his father wanted him to be. Here, for at least this moment, he was exactly who he wanted to be—and it was exactly what *they* wanted from him.

He was probably supposed to say something now; something important; something meaningful to all these people who had opened up their lives to him, and who were all looking at him, waiting. He wanted to tell them that no matter what happened, he was proud to be one of them, and that whether or not he ever found his way home, he would never forget the people of Lykill.

He looked from face to face in the crowd.

"Um," he said. "Thanks. Thanks a lot."

He nodded to Jok, to indicate he was done. Jok motioned

again to the chest. Zack took the key from around his neck.

The key's three stems offered no clues about which one belonged to which lock. Zack looked at Jok again, then at Asleif and Olaf, who stood nearby. None of them moved. He pointed to the lock on the left side of the chest, with the lid marked "Faith."

"Should I try this one?"

"As you see fit, Lost Boy," Jok said.

Zack picked one stem of the key at random and put it into the keyhole. When he tried to turn it, nothing happened. The key wouldn't move. Zack felt heat on the back of his neck.

"I'll just, uh, try another one."

He held out another key stem. The key began to vibrate softly in his hand. This had to be it. He put the key into the hole. It turned easily with a soft click. All at once, the vibrating increased. Everyone seemed to stop breathing. With one more look around, Zack pulled out the key, lifted the lid, and looked inside.

Unlike the outside of the chest, the inside looked as if it were brand-new. The burnished wood shone with a soft gleam when the light caught it. The underside of the lid was carved with more of the familiar intertwined lines, like the ones on the key. Amidst the pattern, several sharp peaks were also carved. They looked like some kind of mountains.

But the compartment itself was bare.

"There's nothing here," Zack said. The words sounded wrong as he said them. After all this, it didn't seem possible.

People in the crowd exchanged puzzled looks. Jok stood up and looked inside. His eyebrows knitted together.

"Open the next one," he said.

Zack fit the key into the middle lock and lifted the second lid, marked "Courage." It, too, was covered with similar carvings on the underside. This section of carving was scored over with wavy lines, as if to indicate smoke or fog. In the center was a circular groove cut deep into the wood. But the second chamber was as empty as the first.

Without prompting, Zack opened the lid marked "Sacrifice" to find the third chamber empty as well. The carvings showed a wall of some sort with a peaked roof and several curved lines extending away from it in an arc; but that was all.

The entire chest was empty.

No one spoke for a full minute. Many of the faces in the crowd had gone from curious to frightened. One or two people began to cry; many put their arms around each other's shoulders and leaned their heads against one another.

"But it's impossible," Jok said. His bass voice was as soft as it had ever been. "The prophecy . . ."

"How can it be empty?" Asleif asked, her eyes wide in disbelief. "Everything seemed to happen as the prophecy said it would."

"Wait!" Zack blurted out, staring into the chest. All three parts of the lid were standing open. Each of the three sections had its distinct features, but the curving twisted lines, or branches, united it all into one continuous image.

Everything seemed to flow from and around the circular groove in the middle.

"Is something?" Olaf said, staring closely at the carving.

Zack held out the key.

Circular. Same size. It should fit. . . .

Without speaking, he started to place the key flat against the round groove in the middle of the chest's lid. The key pulled with the force of a strong magnet toward the chest. It snapped out of Zack's hand and clicked into place like the last piece of a jigsaw puzzle.

Almost immediately, a soft glow came from underneath the key. The twisting, curving lines carved into the chest began to fill with a pale golden light. The light flowed outward from the center and broke into three streams, each one seeming to come from a different stem of the key. Zack watched transfixed as the streams followed three crisscrossing paths until the entire carving in the lid of the chest was filled with a bright golden maze of light. Each of the three streams ended in one of the three sections.

Zack looked around and saw the glow playing like sunlight on dozens of bewildered faces. He looked back at the chest and put his hand to the key again to ensure he could understand what everyone was saying.

"What is it?" Sven asked.

Zack stared at it. The words fell out of his mouth before he even realized he knew the answer. "It's a map."

"A map," several people echoed. No one seemed sure.

"But a map of what?" Jok asked.

175

"This chest is made from the wood of the tree, Yggdrasil, right?" Zack said. "This carving is a map of Yggdrasil itself." The realization was like suddenly waking up. It seemed so clear now. The key's three stems pointed in three directions, like a compass. "Look. The key has three stems. And Yggdrasil has—"

"Three roots," Jok said. "Of course."

Jok used his finger to trace the three paths of light. He spoke almost as if in a trance: "Yggdrasil's Chest, Yggdrasil's Key, And Lost Boy will unite as three, Beginning then the glory quest, That opens with Yggdrasil's Chest." Several others joined in as he quoted the prophecy.

Jok looked at Zack, and continued. "With the key there comes a price, Courage, Faith, and Sacrifice. The way is far, the road will bend, The Boy will lead until the end."

"Until the end," Zack repeated. "We thought this was the end. So what does it mean?"

"It means," Jok said, "that the glory quest has begun, not ended. It means that whatever treasures this chest holds—" he thumped it on its side— "are waiting for us to find them." His round cheeks were balled up in a widening smile. "It means we have places to go."

It was all falling into place. Three chambers, three treasures, and now, three destinations. "Down Yggdrasil's Roots," Zack said.

"Yes," Jok answered. "To Jotunheim, to Niflheim, and even to Asgard, I suppose."

These were the places the Free Man had told him about.

The land of giants, the land of the dead, and the home of the gods.

People were nodding and whispering. The crowd was growing lively again.

"So there must be a way down Yggdrasil's roots. Or along them," Sven said. "Some way of getting there."

"Of course there is," Jok said. "There has to be."

"And then what?" Zack asked.

"Adventure!" Harald yelled.

"Conquest!" Lars shouted.

"Glorrrrrryyyyyy!" Jok boomed. Everyone let up a renewed cheer.

"What about Erik and the Bears?" Zack said. "Don't you think they'll still be coming after us?"

"All the more reason to stay alert and keep moving," Jok said.

"But first—" Sven said.

"FEAST!" everyone called out at once. The crowd quickly took up the chant. "Feast! Feast! Feast! Feast!"

With one giant mood swing, the entire village seemed to decide to worry about the rest of the quest later, and what to eat right away.

Zack found that the key could be easily removed from its place in the chest. The light faded when he took the key back, but the map was still clear.

He kept the key with him as the party stretched into the night. Yggdrasil's Chest was brought inside and set in the middle of a long table with the lid open.

Zack sat, staring at the map for hours. The chest had been his biggest hope for some clue about getting home again. Now it seemed to be launching him farther and farther away. Maybe getting home again wasn't in the cards after all. Maybe this just went on forever.

He pushed at his food. Even if it had been a hot meatloaf sandwich with mashed potatoes and gravy, a side of chili cheese fries, and a pint of mud pie ice cream for dessert, he wouldn't have been hungry for it tonight.

"You look far away," Asleif said. She had been playing music all night and had just come over to sit next to him.

"It's nothing," Zack said. "I was just thinking about some people from home." It was strange to have people who were—in many ways—so close to his father, Ollie, Ashley, and everyone else all around him. Somehow it made the real ones seem farther away.

"Are you going back there?" she asked. "Back where you came from?"

Zack smiled weakly. "I don't know. I was kind of wondering that myself."

"Why? Is it far away?"

"That's a really good question," he said. "I'm not even sure."

Asleif smiled back but Zack could tell she had no idea what he was talking about.

That's all right. Neither do I.

More and more people crowded into the longhouse as the wind kicked up outside. Snow blew in the door when anyone went in or out. Jok and Valdis stoked up the fire in the hearth as high as it would go. As the storm grew outside, the crowd of people grew inside. Soon there was nothing to eat.

"Meat, more!" Olaf called out. He had been given a place of honor, on his own little bed next to the hearth.

"Yes!" Lars called out. "More meat!" He threw an arm around Harald's shoulder and led a chant.

"More! Meat! More! Meat!"

Soon everyone was chanting, but no one wanted to go to the storage shed through the brewing storm.

"We'll wrestle to see who goes to the shed!" Sven shouted.

"Not in my house you won't," Valdis yelled back.

"We'll starve!" Lars moaned dramatically, pretending to stumble and fall onto Zack's shoulder.

"I'll get it!" Zack yelled, and everyone cheered. "For a bunch of Vikings, you guys can be huge babies sometimes."

Several people started bawling and crying like infants, followed by blasts of raucous laughter.

"I'll come with you," Asleif said.

"That's okay," Zack said. "It's pretty nasty outside. Besides, I just need to think a little bit."

"All right," she said. "Thank you. For everything." She planted a small kiss on his cheek. The screams of delight that went up inside the longhouse were louder than anything Zack had heard all day, on or off the battlefield.

He pushed outside. For a brief moment the freezing wind felt good on his flushed face. The storage shed was just beyond the village square. He could see its shadowed outline from Jok's front door. Zack wished for a torch, but with the whipping wind, it wasn't worth going back for one.

He set out in a straight line toward the shed. The snow closed around him as he moved. He reached Jok's gate and felt his way through it, hoping that he was still moving in the right direction. After only a few steps, it began to seem like an impossible task.

He turned back toward the longhouse. As he turned, something low and swift caught him at the knees. It moved by quickly. He never even saw it, and he fell twisting to the ground.

He jumped up and turned quickly all around to make sure nothing else was coming at him. For all he knew, the Bears had sailed right to Lykill. Maybe they were under attack.

"Hey!" He yelled as loud as he could, but knew no one inside would hear him over the wind. He stood still, waiting for another hit, but it didn't come. Now the problem was finding his way back. He was no longer sure which way the storage shed was, much less the longhouse. He took a few steps forward, trying to feel for Jok's gate, but only found air and blowing snow. He tried in the other direction with no luck.

"Oh, man," he said out loud. "This is just like—" Then he stopped.

He stood frozen in place for a moment. The key was heating up against his chest. It quickly grew warmer until it was so hot he had to take it off and hold it with his sleeves over his hands.

This is it! I must be going back again. Back home.

At least . . . I hope I am.

His heart pounded. He couldn't move anywhere in the blinding storm; he could only hope that it was leading toward somewhere he wanted to go.

After several minutes of nothingness, he noticed a growing light. It was as if the storm was continuing, but somewhere the sun was coming out.

Slowly, he could see a little farther in front of him. A large shadowy lump came into view. It looked vaguely familiar. Zack stepped toward it. Another few steps and he would be able to touch it.

A pickup truck. It was a blue pickup truck. It was just a truck, but to Zack's eyes it looked like something incredibly futuristic. He almost wanted to kiss it.

The wind began to die down. Beyond the truck, he saw, was an old beat-up sedan, and more cars beyond that.

He was in a parking lot. A big, beautiful, modern-day parking lot. As the snow slowed, the tall walls of the Metrodome came into view.

Zack felt as though he were in slow motion, trying to take everything in. People were getting out of their cars. Most of them were headed toward the stadium. No one was wearing a helmet or carrying a sword.

A couple passed him, holding hands and laughing. "That was a freaky little storm, wasn't it?"

Zack smiled.

It sure was.

He wondered suddenly how long Jok's tribe would wait until they came looking for him. They were going to be waiting a long time for that meat.

Then, like hitting a wall, he thought about Jock, his father. What day was this? Would Jock be crazy looking for him?

He moved in a daze back toward the Winnie's usual parking spot. What if it wasn't there? Maybe it was five years since he had left the twenty-first century.

"Ayyyy!" Jock Gilman yelled. Zack heard his father's voice before he actually saw him. The familiar sound of it was like a lifeline pulling him the rest of the way in. He really was home.

Jock stepped down from the Winnie, his bare chest still emblazoned with a purple "M." "Where's the bratwurst, huh? You're not going to let a little snow stop you, right? And what's that?" His father pointed at Zack's hand.

Zack looked down. He was still carrying the key. It was once again rusted and dirty, probably twelve hundred years older than the last time he had looked at it.

"It's, uh . . ." Zack had so many thoughts flying through his head, it was hard to choose one. "It's just something I, uh . . ." He trailed off and stared at his father. It was as if in the last fifteen minutes, Jok the Viking had ducked out of the ninth century, changed clothes, cut his hair, and snuck around to meet Zack on the other side as Jock the father.

At the same time, it felt like months since he had seen Jock. He knew he had missed his father while he had been gone. But now he knew just how much.

"What's with the big grin?" Jock asked.

Zack shook his head to jar himself loose. Everything was just as he had left it. All the guys were there—Harlan, Larry, Smitty, Swan—and all of them were looking at Zack expectantly. Somehow, they looked funny without the long beards.

"It's nothing," Zack said. "I'm just, um . . . glad to see you." Without thinking, he lunged forward and wrapped his arms around his dad, holding him tightly. Jock, obviously taken off guard, didn't react for a second—then returned the hug, letting out a surprised laugh.

Jock pulled back and squinted at Zack. "What's going on? Everything okay?"

"Yeah, fine," Zack said. He didn't even know where to begin to explain. Not to mention how quickly they would probably lock him up if he even tried.

"Give me one second," he said. He ran to the back of the Winnie and shoved the key deep into his backpack. He'd think about that later.

Then he took off again for the bratwurst wagon. The brats were still warm by the time he got back.

❧

When the Minnesota Vikings beat the Chicago Bears that afternoon, Zack was hardly surprised. Zack, Jock, and the guys were once again piled into the Winnie, listening to the game on a boom box. The Vikings managed a bit of quick defense, turned the play around, and ran a final game-winning touchdown with less than a minute to go.

"Did you hear that?" Jock yelled, standing up with fists in the air. "Did you hear that? That's the play, just like I said they should do. They can call it what they want, but that's a—

"Gilman Fake," Zack and Jock said at the same time.

Without thinking about it, Zack stepped up and belly-bumped Jock. Jock bumped him in return and wrapped an arm around him in a hug.

"That's the first time you've ever done that," Jock said into his ear. When they separated, Zack saw a little tear in the corner of his father's eye.

Life in the twenty-first century was the sweetest it had ever been, and Zack hadn't even left the Metrodome parking lot. He mowed through two large bags of chips and drank his own six-pack of root beer before the postgame party was over. Watching his father arm wrestle with Smitty, he couldn't keep himself from cheering Jock on. It was still him—it was still Jock Gilman, the man who lived for football and didn't quite understand his own kids. But Zack felt as if somehow, he was looking at a different guy. He just couldn't get over how happy he was to see him, despite all the same old embarrassing stuff. He never would have thought he could miss his dad so much. And the weirdest part was, he hadn't even realized just how much he'd missed him until right now.

Zack's thoughts were interrupted when Jock pinned Smitty and Swan reached out to give Zack a high-five, sending a sharp pain through Zack's hand. All the guys were still celebrating, so no one noticed him look down and see the scar that ran up his palm. It marked his hand exactly where he had touched the red-hot sword blade in Jok's forge. And it sent his mind spinning right back to the ninth century.

Zack excused himself to the back of the Winnie. Facing away from the others, he opened his pack again and stared at the key. He pulled out a pad and started madly writing and sketching. It was like trying to capture a dream on the morning after. Little details were already slipping away from him. He drew a re-creation of the map from Yggdrasil's Chest and wrote down as much of the prophecy as he could remember.

. . . the Boy will lead until the end.

But what did "the end" mean, now that he was gone from there? Erik the Horrible was down but not out. The Bears of the North would no doubt be back with a vengeance. They would want the chest, and the key, and Asleif, too.

Jok's tribe would be vulnerable without the key. Zack felt a twinge of guilt—what if something happened to them because he was gone? He was finally back with his dad, and he'd see Ollie again soon. He should be relieved. And he was, mostly. But now he wondered what was happening to Jok, and Olaf, and . . . Asleif. He missed them just like he'd missed the people *here* when he was back *there*. But it was impossible to know how this was all supposed to play out.

What was Zack's role in the prophecy now that he had come back to the twenty-first century?

Jock's voice hammered back at him from the front of the Winnie. "Hey, what are you doing back there, anyway?"

"Nothing," Zack called, closing his pad.

"You always look like you're thinking about something else," his father said, half to him and half to his friends. Larry, Harlan, and Swan all laughed.

"It's true," Larry said. "Zack, what you need is a little less thinking and a little more action!"

"A little fire in the belly," Jock said, for the millionth time.

"Exactly," Swan said.

Zack sighed. Some things never changed. Too bad they didn't have instant replay in the ninth century. He would have loved to have seen his father's face glimpsing Zack in action.

After all the guys had gone, Jock fired up the Winnie. "Batten down the hatches, Zack. We're heading home."

Zack lumbered back to the front and sat down in the passenger seat next to his father.

"So, did you have a good time?" Jock asked.

Zack paused. "Um . . . yeah. Very interesting time, definitely. How about you?"

Jock thumped himself on the chest and held out a purple-stained hand. "Absolutely. Any time the Vikings win, it's a good day. Right?"

"Right," Zack said. He reached over, and they shook on it.

EPILOGUE

Orn writhed and screamed as Ogmunder the Wizard bent over him on the examining table.

"Oh, be quiet," Erik snapped. "It's just an arm. Stop your sniveling."

Ogmunder turned the pages of a large book. "Hmmmm, let's see," he mused tentatively. "New arm, new arm . . ."

Erik sidled up to the wizard. "We need to hurry this up. I've got business to the south of here."

"Oh?" said the wizard, crushing seed pods into a clay jar.

"Actually, it may be something that interests you," Erik said. Orn's screams had gone to whimpers, but they, too, were ignored.

"I'm listening," Ogmunder said without looking up from his potion. He pulled a live mouse from a cage. He dropped it into the jar and poured a thick black liquid over it.

"You know about the Lost Boy? The prophecy?"

"Everyone knows the prophecy," the wizard said.

"Do you know that the Lost Boy has been found?"

"I had heard."

"And do you know that he is lost again?"

Ogmunder stopped mixing. He turned his head slowly to face Erik.

Erik continued. "Yes. Word gets around quickly. Jok of Lykill is not the only one with spies, of course."

Ogmunder raised an eyebrow. "And what does this mean for me?"

"Well," Erik said. "Maybe nothing. But then again, it could mean a share in the contents of Yggdrasil's Chest."

"But you already said that Jok of Lykill has opened the chest."

"And it was found empty."

Ogmunder dropped his mixing jar and it shattered on the floor. The mouse he had stirred into the potion skittered away through a hole in the wall. The rest of the ingredients spilled across the dirt floor.

Orn moaned weakly. "Not again . . ."

"Did you say it was empty?" Ogmunder whispered.

Erik was beginning to move around the room, pacing like a cat. His torch trailed a high flame as he went. "There are three things I want more than anything in this world. I want to see Jok of Lykill and his ridiculous tribe beg for mercy. I want to squash that Lost Boy like a worm under my thumb. And I want Yggdrasil's Treasure." He looked brightly at Ogmunder. "Soon I'll have the first, and the other two will follow."

Ogmunder leaned in close. "What is your plan?"

"It has already begun," Erik said. "Jok will either spend his time looking for the Lost Boy or go directly for the treasure. What he doesn't know is that either way, he is sailing straight into our path. The trap has been set."

A slow smile crept over Ogmunder's face. "Go on."

Erik paced to the mouth of the cave and back, speaking quickly. "Within a few days, I'll have Jok and his men in chains. When I'm through, you can use them for spare body parts, for all I care. And if the Lost Boy knows what's good for him, he'll stay away. But if I'm lucky, he'll come sniffing around and I'll get to see him burn."

Ogmunder nodded, but was otherwise very still. "And then of course there's the small matter of Yggdrasil's Treasure."

Erik turned to him, his face set and steady. "The prophecy has begun. The chest has been opened. With Jok out of the way, the missing treasure will be ours for the taking. And you, my friend, can help me find it." The corners of his mouth turned up slightly as he went on. "I will bend the world to its knees, you will have anything you've ever wanted, and everyone will be happy."

"What about me?!" Orn cried out. "What about my arm?"

Erik looked at him with a sneer. "Yes, yes. One thing at a time." He looked up at Ogmunder again. "One thing at a time. Don't you agree?"

The sounds of their howling laughter echoed through Ogmunder's cave and out into the still of the night air.

⚘

Look for the next exciting Viking adventure, QUEST FOR FAITH, in stores now!

Zack is back in ninth-century Scandinavia once again. Now well aware of his bizarre role among the Vikings, he's on his way to the mysterious Jotunheim, land of the giants, in search of the object that will fulfill the first of his duties as the legendary "Lost Boy." Only, this time, he's on his own: Jok and his crew have been kidnapped by Erik the Horrible.

Zack has no idea exactly where Jotunheim is or what he'll do when he gets there, but he knows he must get there soon, or risk losing his Viking friends—and the treasure—forever.